All Our Troubles

James D. Farrell

Oh, Ireland my first and only love

Where Christ and Caesar are hand in glove

James Joyce

CONTENT

ELLAN VANNIN

Government Offices, Dublin, Late 1960s

Bumper Mc Sheehy paced up and down the thickly carpeted floor of his large oak-panelled office chomping on a Cuban cigar, a portrait of the ever-watchful Eamon De Valera hanging above the beautiful green-tinged Connemara marble Georgian fireplace. In one hand, a Waterford crystal glass half full of Hennessy brandy, in the other a rolled-up newspaper. "Fuckers, that's what they are –fuckers. If they think they can get rid of old Bumper Mc Sheehy that easy I'll show them, so I will." He stubbed out his cigar, swallowed his drink in one gulp, and pressed the intercom button. "Miss Maloney, get hold of the Minister of Defence for me like a good girl, tell him to get his fat arse over here pronto, you`ll find him in Delaney's or some other feckin` pub around the town."

Thirty minutes later the Minister of Defence entered and sat opposite his boss without speaking. Martin Prendergast was a stocky, well-dressed man in his late fifties; he had spent his early career as an officer in the Irish Army before entering politics. Well educated, a Belvedere and Trinity College man, with a deep love of literature and all things pertaining to politics and military history, but also renowned for his direct manner which at times could be very direct indeed. "Prendergast, have you seen today's papers they're trying to crucify me, a shower of fuckers that`s what they are, out to get me just like my father, I give my life to the country and look what happens. Have yeh seen the latest polls for Christ's sake, our support is at an all-time low, I'd have been better off staying at home on the farm. Anyway, Prendergast, you're the expert on everything aren't yeh now clever clogs, so tell me what can we do and for fuck sake give it to me straight?" The minister sat forward hands-on desk and clearing his throat replied. "Well, Prime Minister, if you want an honest opinion it's like this, we can do nothing, we`re fucked. The games up for the government and that`s that." He stood abruptly and turned to leave. "Jesus Christ, stay where you are, Prendergast, you're going nowhere in a hurry, I'm tellin` yeh now. I put you where you are and you're not walking out on me, not in my time of need. Now sit down and give me some answers, there must be a way out of this awful bloody mess; there must be something we can do?" "Boss, the situation is simple, unemployment is sky-high, emigration is endemic and the farming industry has all but collapsed thanks to European intervention, but these difficulties we can overcome in one way or another, however, Prime Minister, the insurmountable problem for the government, the killer for us is the black north, the never-ending fuckin` problem of Northern Ireland. I blame the British and especially that fucker Edward Carson for the whole mess and him a Dublin man, an Irish speaker, and they say he was a great hurler. Do you know, boss, on his death bed he confessed to his wife Ruby he'd made a fatal mistake regarding the partitioning of Ireland and by fuck was he right, the problems he`s caused for the past fifty years with his bloody partition. That's his fuckin' legacy alright, crucifying the queer fella Wilde and fuckin' up the country? Jasus, there's not a man, woman, or child in Ireland and further afield who hasn't suffered in one way or another because of Carson and his artificial border?" Then Mountbatten goes and partitions' India leaving a legacy of bitterness just like the north. Then they partition Palestine causing the same fuckin' problems over and over again. Do the Brits never learn that partition doesn't works, and always done to appease a minority and their threat of violence." "Yes, Prendergast, yes you're right and things are getting worse by the day sure look what's happening in Belfast with the Catholic people burned out of their homes by raging Protestant mobs led by the B Specials while the R.U.C. and army stand by and watch. Yesterday, they tried to burn down a chapel and monastery and what are we doing down here, nothing. We have to get the Northern Ireland Government suspended; they won't listen to reason. If only they would bring in power sharing and give Catholics their say, grant everyone equal rights and we wouldn't be in the mess we are now. Instead, they use force against civil rights protesters and I've tried to speak to the unionist politicians but they won't take my calls. I've put pressure on the British to take control of the situation, sure didn't I speak to Wilson last week and while the labour government is sympathetic they won't act in case there's a unionist backlash. If we could only get rid of Stormont and let the Brits take over at least that way we'd have a chance of ending the violence against nationalists. The eyes of the world are on us and we're sitting doing nothing and that's why the people are so against us, we have to save the country. Jesus, Prendergast, you're the Minister of Defence tell me why are we doing nothing, why are we sitting on our arses waiting for the powder keg to explode. We have to do something-anything at all. Anything to get rid of Stormont and the only thing unionists understand is violence; sure the fuckers even support apartheid in South Africa." "Listen now, boss, calm down a minute," the minister replied, "there's nothing we can do, nothing at all, our hands are tied, didn`t I explain it all loud and clear at the last cabinet meeting. For Christ's sake, boss, did yeh not listen to a word I said?" Bumper sat back and responded in a low voice. "Doing nothing is not an option, minister, we`ll go down in history as losers, a total failure as a government and we can't let that happen, can we. Could we not make an incursion into Northern Ireland even for a few hours, anything to force the Brits into action?" "Boss," the minister replied firmly, "do you know how many British soldiers are stationed in the north, well I'll tell you now, over twelve thousand. There's the R.U.C, thirteen thousand of the fuckers armed to the teeth, and what about the special constabulary the B- Specials. Any form of military action is impossible, boss, out of the question." "You left something out, minister." Bumper replied sarcastically. "And what's that now, boss?" "Prendergast, you never mentioned the A- Specials, the C-Specials, and the D- Specials, all thirty thousand of them, the list goes on and on. Jesus Christ, minister, how many special constabularies do they have in the north, a fucking A-Z of special constables, the alphabet constabulary that's what they should be called, are they expecting a fuckin`German invasion or what. Tell me now, Prendergast, how many men do we have in the army?" "Well, boss, I don't know the answer to that; nobody knows it changes every week. At the moment about two thousand men although over a quarter are off on long-term sickness." "And what sort of sickness do these men have?" "An embarrassing and debilitating illness, boss, piles, they're a big problem in the army." "Piles, minister, what the fuck are yeh talking about what the fuck do yeh mean by piles." "Haemorrhoids, boss, it's the medical term." "Tell me now, minister, why are piles such a big problem in the army?" "Well, to be honest now, boss, that's a sore point, so it is, but primarily a bad diet and lack of exercise are the cause." "But, minister, can the army doctors do nothing to help the soldiers." "Well, boss, they have tried the bum cream, but it's not effective as the men are suffering from what is termed deep piles. Jasus, you should see them on the parade ground, the state of the poor lads and them scratching away like mad, a terrible sight to behold and the reason why so many are off on long term sick." "Jesus, Prendergast, we have an army and there must be some fit soldiers, how many fit men could we muster." "Well, boss, it isn't strictly about the manpower; it's more about the equipment or in our case the lack of equipment that's the problem." "Jesus, Prendergast, we have an army so we must have guns, bombs, and trucks, and the like do we not?" "Yes, boss, we have guns but they're in terrible condition, barely useable, you see they got a lot of rough treatment during the war." "What war are yeh talking about for Christ's sake?" "The civil war, boss." "But, Prendergast, the civil war ended over forty years ago, did we never update the weapons for the army?" "No, boss, why would we there was never the need to spend money on modern weapons when there's no chance of us going to war and to be honest now, boss, who the fuck would want a war with us. But, hold on a minute we do have a few excellent weapons, the ones we captured from the I.R.A. during the border campaign of the fifties and I'll give those I.R.A. fellows their dues they kept their guns in a first-class condition, we could learn a thing or two from those lads." "But, minister; surely we have trucks and bombs?" "Well, boss, the trucks are clapped out after all the driving over bomb cratered roads during the invasion." "Hold on, Prendergast, invasion of what, what are yeh talking about?" "The D- Day invasion, boss, the trucks carried troops all over Europe." "What the fuck are you on about, minister, have yeh lost the plot or what?" "No, boss, no, we bought the trucks off the British Army after the Second World War and bejesus we got some bargain, dirt cheap so they were. The only problem is not one of them would take you as far as Dundalk." By this time, a dejected Bumper sat, hands-on head, and leaning forward inquired. "And what about bombs, do we even have a few little bombs we could use; surely to God we have a few bombs lying around?" "Boss, I told you before we don't have any wars, so why in God's name would we need bombs, besides the army used up all the bombs at the massacre down in Cork." Bumper jumped to his feet. "Jesus H. Christ," he shouted, "what massacre are yeh fuckin` talking about, Prendergast, were any civilians hurt?" "No, boss, no, of course not, it was during the civil war when the army rounded up a few of the irregulars and blew them up, although it`s strange how things turned out. At the time, we were the irregulars under Dev and the regulars were under Michael Collins before we became the regulars, if you get my drift. Anyway, they blew up our boys and used up all the bombs, and isn't it amazing the way things turned out in the end, truly amazing." "What are yeh talking about, Prendergast; I don't understand what you mean." "Well, boss, it was like this, one day we`re terrorists or irregulars under Dev. and the next day we`re regulars running the government, and in fairness now I'd put it all down to little Willie Cosgrave the Prime Minister at the time." "But, what's little Willie got to do with all this?" "Boss, it's one of the defining moments of our recent history and here's the story." "Our lot under Dev. were waging civil war on the government over the signing of the Treaty Agreement, and during the war Dev. started to shoot government ministers. When, against all the odds, we go and win the general election and when Dev. turns up at the government buildings to take over as Prime Minister isn't little Willie Cosgrove waiting for him to hand over power. Now, boss, you can imagine how Cosgrove felt with Dev. having killed many of his close friends and colleagues, and as Dev. approaches little Willie`s bodyguard reaches for his gun and says to Cosgrave, Sir, do I shoot or salute. Cosgrave thought about it for a few seconds and ordered his bodyguard to salute Dev. his bitter enemy and that's where we are today, but sure it`s all behind us now thanks be to God." "Jesus, Prendergast, you're one boring fucker so yeh are, where do you get all this information from, Christ man it's no wonder your wife left yeh, but back to business. Tell me this now, what`s the point of having an army if we've no equipment?" "Boss, with the greatest of respect you're not correct on this one, what we have is not strictly an army, is it now?" "Well, what the hell is it, Prendergast, the fuckin` boy scouts." The minister threw his head back laughing loudly. "Come on now, boss, and don't be ridiculous, what we have is not an army but more correctly a defence force. The official title is The Irish Defence Force and that's what we are." "But defending what, Prendergast, if I may ask?" "The barracks, boss - the British Army barracks, it was part of the Treaty Agreement. At the time nobody envisaged the nascent Irish Free State surviving more than a year or two, so we promised the British we would guard the barracks and keep them nice and tidy in case they ever returned." "So, minister, you're telling me we have an army to guard old English barracks." "Well, I suppose that's one way of looking at it, to stop vandals stealing the lead off the roofs and destroying the military structures. Their fine examples of military architecture, lovely red brick, slated buildings, and the British excelled at building barracks all over the world, so we do have an obligation to look after them. But to be fair, boss, we don't only guard the barracks you're forgetting about the bins and buses." "What about the bins and buses, Prendergast?" "Well, boss, when the bin men or busmen go on strike, which is frequent these days, we step in to lift the bins or provide transport for the public. So, you can see the importance of us having a defence force especially when the unions call a strike?" "But, hold on now, Prendergast, I hope you're not spinning me a yarn, did yeh not say the trucks were all clapped out, so how do they replace the buses during the strikes?" "Yes, boss, they are knackered but okay for short trips in and out of the city, but not any long-haul stuff." "Listen, Prendergast, I hear what you're saying, but there's something I don't understand What about the troops we sent to Katanga in the Congo with the United Nations a couple of years ago, didn't I inspect them myself at Casement Aerodrome before they went to Africa. A fine body of men they were too, all smartly dressed in well-pressed summer uniforms and armed with brand new black shiny rifles, those weapons were certainly not from the civil war to be sure, Jesus I hope you're not trying to pull the wool over my eyes, minister?" No, boss, no, I would never do that would I now, everything I've told you is true. Anyway, boss, I've been meaning to speak to you about an important matter." "And what's that now, Prendergast, come on spill the beans." "Boss, has the Swedish Ambassador tried to contact you at all." "No, minister, why the fuck would he want to contact me." "Well, it's a sensitive matter, boss, a very sensitive matter indeed." Prendergast turned to avoid eye contact. "It`s nothing at all, boss, just the small matter of the missing rifles." "What missing rifles are yeh talking about, minister, Jasus; does nobody tell me anything around here?" "Eh," he continued, "the ones we borrowed for the African trip." "What, we borrowed rifles from the Swedes?" "Yes, boss, and that`s the whole truth of it." "But, why, Prendergast, why?" "Boss, the United Nations asked us to send a contingent of Irish troops to the Congo, but as I've told you we hadn't got the proper equipment. However, the Swedes kindly offered us a loan of their surplus weapons if we agreed to do the dangerous jungle patrols and they did guard duty they thought it would be safer for their men to keep them out of harm's way." "And why didn't we give them their guns back?" "Eh, we lost them in the jungle, boss." "Holy Christ, Prendergast, how the fuck did we lose the guns in the jungle." "Well, to be correct, boss, we didn't exactly lose them; they were robbed by the Balubas." "Who the fuck are the Balubas, Prendergast, tell me now?" "The Balubas are the blackies who live in the jungle in Katanga in the Congo, the fuckers who robbed the guns. The Balubas are terrorists, the same ones that ambushed and massacred our boys, and to make matters worse didn't the dirty robbin` bastards steal the Swedish rifles." "Have you tried to get them back?" "Of course, boss, of course we did, didn't we write a strongly worded letter to the chief of the Balubas in the jungle, however we never got a reply, but to tell the truth the chief most likely couldn't understand the Irish language." Bumper jumped to his feet and banged his fist on the table. "What the fuck, are you telling me you sent a letter written in Irish to the chief of the Balubas in the jungle, Prendergast, are yeh out of your fuckin` mind, are yeh thick or what?" "No, boss, no," he responded face reddened by the insult, "army protocol, boss, it couldn't be helped. Dev. issued a decree stating all army correspondence must be in the Irish language." Bumper thundered over to the drinks cabinet pouring large measures of brandy into two tumblers. "Jesus, I`ve heard it all now, so I have, no wonder this country is all fucked up. Prendergast, will you sort out the Swedish Ambassador like a good man, my plate`s full at the moment the way things are around here." "Consider it done, boss, case closed, I'll sort everything out." "Prendergast, one thing I'm curious about. Those smart summer uniforms the men were wearing at Casement Aerodrome, did we get them from the Swedes as well?" "No, boss, no," the minister replied smiling, "they were World War Two, German desert uniforms from Rommel's African Corps. who fought at El- Alamein? We got them cheap from Hector Gray`s second-hand shop off Henry Street, you know the place. He sells surplus army gear and bejesus, boss, we got a great deal; he even dry cleaned the uniforms for free." "Okay, Prendergast, I don't want to hear any more of this bullshit now let's get down to business. As I've said, we have to do something about the situation in Northern Ireland, doing nothing is not an option for the government. Listen, could we not even rustle up a handful of fit men and get them up to the north by train, coach, or even taxi. Make an incursion, capture a customs post on the British side on the border, and hold it for a few days to get the attention of the world's press. It would be an international affair and the U.N. would become involved and we could force the Stormont issue." "Sorry, boss, the out-of-hours working is a problem for the army, the men would have to agree, and it would cost us a fortune in overtime. The problem is the army trade union, a very militant bunch pardon the pun. The Department of Defence has struck a deal with the union, nine to five working hours only with double time for holidays and out of hours and the men have to agree to nights and weekends." "Jesus, Prendergast, I don't believe what I'm hearing, it is the fucking boy scouts and not an army." "But, boss, with the greatest of respect, you're not listening to what I'm saying. It's a defence force so why would out-of-hours working or weekends be relevant if yeh get my gist. So, to send them over the border out of hours would cost an arm and a leg and the men wouldn't agree; it would be far too dangerous." "But, hold on a minute, minister, the funeral of the young soldier killed in Katanga, what was his name –Kelly, that's it, Private Paddy Kelly, from out Finglas way was held on a Sunday wasn't it with full military honours and a colour party from the army, how did yeh negotiate that one with the union? Out of hours working, what a load of crap, Prendergast, are yeh taking the mickey out of me." "No, boss, not at all, the colour party at the funeral weren't soldiers they were actors dressed as soldiers, a hell of a lot cheaper and less hassle than trying to deal with the army trade union and all to keep the bloody Yanks happy. Yeh, a strange affair that funeral and Private Kelly's brother, Eddie the Undertaker`s Assistant, anyway the ruse worked well enough until that feckin` journalist from the Evening Herald, Nosey Flynn, cottoned on to the fact the soldiers were actors. One of the soldiers –I mean actors drank in his local pub and spilled the beans. Luckily when Nosey started making noises around the town we told him in the interest of national security to zip it and when that didn't work we had the Horse O Houlihan apply a little torture which fairly shut the fucker up." "What, Prendergast, Holy God, are you telling me we tortured a journalist from the Evening Herald, and who the fuck is the Horse O Houlihan?" "The Horse is the Irish army's official torturer and good at the job, so he is." "Jesus,

Prendergast, I'm like a fuckin` mushroom around here, kept in the dark and fed bullshit, now tell me  what are we going to do about the awful mess we`re in?" The minister sipped his brandy without replying when Bumper exploded in a fit of rage. "Listen, Prendergast, my family the Mc Sheehys were proud people and suffered terribly at the hands of the English, and that fucker what do yeh call him now- the robbin` bastard, Spenser-the poet, Edmund Spenser, do yeh know who I'm talkin` about, minister." "Yes, of course, boss, the famous poet laureate and author of *The Fairy Queen*, I studied him at university, he`s one of England`s greatest poets and I remember my English professor saying *Oh, beautiful Spenser your poetry's so deep when I read your words I fall straight asleep.*" "Well, Prendergast, the poet himself comes into our country and drives my people from their land and occupies our castle at Kilcolman, a place we've lived for centuries on lands given to us by the Irish lords for our devoted service. Moreover, he sits in our castle writing his fuckin` poem *The Fairy Queen* in praise of the bastard heretic Lisa, the English harlot. Robbin` bastards that's what they were, robbin` bastards, and tell me this. What the fuck are they still doing in our country, we never invited them, and they're still up in the north?" "But, boss, don't be ridiculous now; it's not as simple as that. The reality is the majority of people in the six counties regard themselves as British subjects and want to remain so. You cannot force these people to change their minds or leave the country; two wrongs don't make a right. After eight hundred years of colonisation, at least we won back twenty-six counties and that's the reality, force would only make things worse. Someday, when there's a nationalist majority it will be an entirely different matter." Bumper jumped up and banged his fist on the desk. "Force, I'll tell yeh about force, Prendergast. The fuckin` English drove my people out of the Awbeg Valley into the bogs and mountains, off the land we cultivated for centuries and served our Irish masters well, the Mc Carty More and the Desmonds. We were Scottish Gallowglass, warriors of the Gaelic lords, fierce, loyal, and true, and we fertilised the soil of the Awbeg Valley with our blood protecting them, never betraying the Irish for Saxon gold. First, the English come and drive us off our land then the thieving Spenser moves into our castle writing his poetry while we live like the fox and the hare up in hovels on the barren mountains starving to death. Jesus wept, Prendergast, the base ignobility of it all, the utter shame and degradation of my people. Then he writes a lengthy dissertation to the Queen, a solution to the Irish problem. Moreover, do yeh know what his solution was, minister, this Oxford scholar, this cream of English society. Starvation – starve us to death, yes, drive us into a small area and corral us like animals until we were starving and forced to eat each other to survive. I bet they never taught you that at Trinity College, minister. Yes, Spenser's solution was for us to cannibalise each other to solve the Irish problem, but I'll tell you something now; there never was an Irish problem, Prendergast, only a fuckin` English problem and it's still that way today." He stopped in mid-sentence and gulped down his brandy as tears welled in his eyes. "And, minister, they came with the bible in one hand and the sword in the other to exterminate the Irish people.

Genocide, that's what it was in the name of their Lutheran church. Some Christianity with no mention of *love thy neighbour* or *thou shalt not steal*. However, one night we came as the poet laureate stood on the battlements of Kilcolman castle admiring his conquest, bathed in silver moonlight, lute in hand singing the praises of Gloriana his virgin Queen. We came and bejesus, Prendergast, we came all right and make no fuckin` mistake about that. A horde of starving dispossessed people, anatomies of death, and the people of the once noble Clan Mc Sheehy. Yes, Prendergast, we crawled out of our caves and hovels, scrambled down the Ballyhoura Hills, and charged along the Awbeg Valley like a swarm of locusts in the night screaming our war cry *Mc Sitigh Abu, Mc Sitigh Abu* driving the English from our land and killing everyone who didn't speak the native tongue. Now, that's what robbers deserve, Prendergast. Moreover, do yeh know what happened to the high and mighty Elizabethan land-grabbing bastard Spenser? He died in poverty in London destitute the poor man, even Shakespeare was at his funeral. Now there's a lesson to be learned from that, so do yeh expect me to sit here and do nothing about the treatment of my fellow Irishmen and women in the north. Look, Prendergast." He opened a drawer and pulled out a map that he spread across the desk. "Now, minister, tell me what do you see?" "That`s easy, boss, it's a 1:25000 scale A.A. road map of Ireland." "No, man, no, use your feckin` imagination. When I look at the map I see a teddy bear, a cuddly little teddy bear, but the heads missing stolen by the British and I want my teddy bear`s head back." "Boss, for God's sake calm down now or you`ll give yourself a heart attack." "Sorry, Prendergast, I've been under a lot of pressure recently, yes, you're correct, we could never beat the British militarily, and we can never force the Protestants of Northern Ireland into a United Ireland. I just want to do something, anything to help our fellow Catholic Irishmen, and women. Now you go home, Prendergast, and use that educated brain of yours to come up with something, some kind of operation to break the impasse, go on now and don't let me down." "Good night, boss," the minister replied as he departed in the direction of Delaney`s public house.

A week later, he returned to outline his proposals to the Prime Minister for a military operation against Northern Ireland to regain the nation's pride, save the government, and force Britain into suspending Stormont. "Well, Prendergast, what have yeh got for me now?" "Nothing, boss," was the curt reply, "I`ve left no stone unturned, I've met with the Irish Army Council, consulted with experts in the field of military operations. Moreover, most importantly my sources in the north inform me the British have two Vulcan jet fighter bombers on standby at R.A.F. Aldergrove for immediate retaliatory action if we attempt to cross the border. The consensus is simple, very simple indeed. The chances of us launching a military operation against the north is zero-to put it simply and as I've said before loud and clear, we`re fucked." "Prendergast," Bumper Mc Sheehy responded in a low crumbling voice, "I put all my faith in you and I can't believe you let me down, it's the end of the road for us now, it`s all over." "Boss, hold on a minute, anything to do with Northern

Ireland is out of the question and that`s for sure, but I have an idea, an alternative plan that might just do the job." Bumper sprung to his feet and shook the minister's hand vigorously. "Jasus, Martin Prendergast, now you're feckin`talkin,` I knew yeh wouldn't let me down me ould flower, come on now and tell me what this brilliant pal of yours is?" "Right, boss, sit down now and listen to this. We're going to invade the Isle of Man and hold the British to ransom." "Jesus, Prendergast, are yeh fucking mad or what you said it yourself, we haven't got the men or equipment to invade Butlin`s holiday camp at Mosney let alone the fuckin` Isle of Man, sure didn't we hire actors for a colour party in Glasnevin, you told me so yourself. Seriously, I`m going to have to consider your position in the government." "No, boss, hold on a minute, listen to what I have to say, my proposal is far more complex than a military operation that`s only a small part of the plan. The legal position of the Isle of Man is unique. It's a self-governing crown dependency and not part of Great Britain. However, the Queen is Lord of Mann with absolute power; to put it simply she legally owns the island. Now, this is the best part, boss, you'll love this. The Queen's representative on the island is the Lieutenant Governor, Sir Bartley Dunne. Do yeh get it, boss?" "No, I don't fuckin` get it, what in God's name are yeh on about." "Boss, Sir Bartley has executive power on the island as the Queen's representative controlling everything, answering to neither politicians nor the people, and has the executive power to act on the Queen's behalf in her absence and she only visits the island once a year, he has power of attorney to make any decisions regarding the Isle of Man." "And so fuckin` what, Prendergast, I don't see what you're getting at?" "Boss, we invade the island and force, Sir Bartley, on the Queen`s behalf, to sign the island over to the Irish Government." "But what good is the Isle of Man to our government?" "A bargaining tool, boss, we can swop the island for the six counties and if that doesn't work we`ll settle for the suspension of Stormont." "Prendergast, that's fuckin` brilliant, Jasus you're a bright spark alright and there's no doubt about that. Christ, we can come out on top with this one now, boyo, yes, we most certainly can." He rubbed his hands gleefully and filled two tumblers to the brim with brandy. "Here, take this and tell me the full plan I want to know all the details. Slainte, Martin Prendergast, Slainte." "My pleasure, boss, and here's the story. We send fifty men as the invading force over to the island." "But without transport, minister, how do we get them over?" "Now, here's the clever part, boss, the Isle of Man steam packet ferry, over first thing in the morning and back that night, I can even get a ten per cent discount off the normal fare for fifty men." "But, Prendergast, what happens when the Manx see our soldiers, our will men have guns won't they now?" "Yes, of course, boss, this is a proper invasion nothing willy nilly about this operation and of course the men will carry rifles but without ammunition, we don't want anyone getting hurt now do we; this is a peaceful invasion so why would we need ammunition, and here's the plan. We're going to inform the Manx Government we`re making a film, a sequel to *The Longest Day* called *The Longest Night*, so they`ll think our soldiers are actors, what do yeh think, boss?" "Good, minister, so far so good, but what about Sir Bartley Dunne, how do we get him to sign the handover papers?" "Simple, we march to his house and force him to sign. I'll have the Attorney General draw up a tight legal document and make sure there are no loopholes." "But, what if Sir Bartley Dunne, Jasus that's one fuckin` stupid name isn't it, refuses to sign the papers." "Well, in that case, we`ll have to use torture, boss, good old tried and tested torture, we`ll torture the little fucker until he signs the papers." "Christ, Prendergast, what sort of torture do you have in mind?" The minister slapped his hand on the desk and replied laughingly. "Jasus, your funny, boss, there's only one type of torture now and it`s the sort that works and that's why we're putting the Horse O Houlihan on the case. However, boss, it's not your concern, and if you prefer I'll get the Horse to use the funny kind of torture rather than the painful kind." "Prendergast, you're having a laugh aren't you, you`re telling me there's a funny kind of torture." "Yes, boss, and believe it or not it's highly effective and the Horse O Houlihan is an expert at it. You should have seen him work on Nosey Flynn from the Evening Herald and his technique is simple. He starts ticking the feet or tummy until the victim is in hysterics and finds it difficult to breathe and if that doesn't work he takes the gloves off, figuratively speaking, and tickles under the arms and that always does the job, and they do anything for the Horse to stop. No, need for pulling out teeth or any bloody stuff and believe me it works just as well. The Horse finds the feather duster the most effective and by God, you should see him work with the feather duster, boss, it would bring tears from a stone." "I can't believe what I`m hearing,

Prendergast, but I don't like violence and if you get Bartley Dunne to sign this way, that's fine." "But, tell me, Prendergast, why we need to send over soldiers at all?" "Because, in the eyes of the world it has to be a proper invasion, boss. It`s the Republic of Ireland flexing its military muscle; we have to put a spin on the invasion. Look, I've prepared a press statement for the world's media." The statement read:

At sixteen hundred hours Greenwich Mean Time (GMT) on the 28th of July under the cover of darkness, special elite highly trained storm troopers of the Irish Army Rangers Division, supported by units of the Irish Army Auxiliary Pioneers equipped with flame throwers, and by the Irish Navy and Air Force with scattered units of the F.C.A. Covered by a blanket of artillery fire the Irish forces spearheaded an assault on the British occupied Isle of Man as a retaliatory first strike at the British for their continual illegal occupation of the six counties of Ulster and the brutal occupation of Ireland for eight hundred years, so brutal at times we could hardly take it. Under heavy fire from the Manx defence forces, the brave Irish troops captured key installations, raising the Irish tricolour on Mount Snaefell. The Lieutenant Governor of the island Sir Bartley Dunne on the Queen's behalf forced to sign over ownership of the Isle of Man to the Irish Republic. The legal title Lord of Man now lies with the Irish Government; no one was killed or injured in this outstanding military operation. The Irish Government intends to use the island, which was originally under Irish control, as a bargaining tool with the British Government regarding the future of the occupied six counties and for the immediate suspension of Stormont. We also confirm the island is renamed Oilean Mannain thus reverting to its proper Gaelic name until changed by the English.

"Good, Prendergast, very good indeed and I believe your plan might work, and tell me now who's in charge of the operation?" "Well, boss, I think it should be a soldier of low rank, a non-commissioned man and I recommend the Horse O Houlihan for the job, that way we can kill two birds with one stone. He can be the official torturer and the commander; he's an ex-British commando and more than capable of the role. We`ll tell the men nothing, it's a day trip as a reward for their hard work; no overtime but a few free pints and fish and chips on the way home, only the Horse and a couple of corporals will be informed of the operation, do I have your go ahead, boss?" "Yes, minister, you have, and tell me now what will we call the mission?" "Operation Ellan Vannin, boss," he replied. "And tell me, minister, what does Ellan Vannin mean?" "Well, it's what the Manx call the island; however it's a mispronunciation of the proper name Oilean Mannin after the Irish Sea God, Mannain Mc Lir. You see, boss, the Manx language is Irish except certain words are pronounced differently, sort of Irish with an English accent. Where we use *A* they use *Y*. Do you know, boss, the last person who speaks Manx fluently is an elderly gentleman called Ned Madrell. Now, a few years ago when Dev. heard this he requested Sir Bartley Dunne, yes the same one, to record the language for posterity. However,

Dunne refused and Dev. was incensed sending over a ship with R.T.E. equipment and recorded every word of the Manx language before it became extinct and all paid for by the Irish people and what thanks did we get from the high and mighty Bartley Dunne or indeed the Manx people. And do yeh know, boss, the Lieutenant Governor is always an Englishman, they don`t trust a Manx for the job?"

At seven-thirty on a sunny July morning, the invasion force of the Irish Army consisting of fifty men armed with Lee Enfield rifles without ammunition, C rations including six boxes of Tayto cheese and onion crisps, and a dozen flagons of Bulmer's cider for subsistence on their short journey, boarded the Isle of Man steam packet ferry to Douglas. The weather sunny, the sea calm, the trip uneventful. On arrival, the men lined up on the dock two abreast under the command of Sergeant the Horse O Houlihan and two corporals. *Cle- Deis, Cle- Deis -Left Right, Left- Right* ordered the Horse as the men commenced the three-mile march to the governor`s house at Baldrine. The first unusual thing occurred when two young girls asked for autographs followed by the local police saluting much to the amusement of the soldiers. After half an hour's marching at a blistering pace the men complained of thirst, and the sergeant stopping at a sleepy country public house *The Ochan Arms* led the men into the beer garden and barked to a startled barman. "Okay, pal, gimme fifty pints of the local beer and make it snappy, we haven't got all day." After a few pints, the men settled in, smoking, chatting, drinking pint after pint of Okells the local beer before the singing began. All the old rebel songs got a rendition. *Kevin Barry, James Connolly, Follow me up to Carlow.* While the men partied the Horse O Houlihan ordered a taxi and travelled to sir Bartley Dunne`s mansion. "Stop here and wait for me, pal, I'll only be a few minutes," he instructed the taxi driver, strolled up the tree-lined driveway to the fancy-looking house, and rang the doorbell. A minute later, a small bald man opened the door. "Can I help you, sir," the man inquired, but without replying, the sergeant rushing in slammed the door behind him pushing the startled man into the living room and shouted. "I am, Sergeant the Horse O Houlihan of the army of the Irish Republic, here today to demand you sign these papers on behalf of Queen Elizabeth the Second of the United Kingdom transferring the title Lord of Mann and ownership of the island to the Irish Government." "But, sir," the bald man responded, "I must protest, you`re making a big mistake." The sergeant grabbed the man by the throat. "Listen, pal, and listen good do yeh hear me now, don't yeh ever interrupt me when I'm speaking or I'll have to be givin` yeh the slap and tickle torture, so I will, and that'll make yeh cry like a feckin`baby, yeh baldy fucker. For eight hundred years, two months and five days and," he checked his watch, "six minutes to be exact, you English have oppressed the Irish people, whipped us, shot us, starved us, yeh raped the men and then the women and dat`s only the start, I could go on and on but it`s far too shocking. Yes, dat`s what yeh did to us yeh baldy English fuck face, but things are going to change and from now on we`re the boss." "But, sir," the man rasped, "there's something important I have to tell you. I`m not Sir Bartley Dunne, his lordship is at his holiday home in the south of France, he and Lady Georgina spend the summer there, I'm only the butler." The sergeant stopped dead in his tracks. "Jasus, why didn't yeh tell me dat in the first place instead of wastin` me fuckin` time, when`s the governor due back?" "The end of September, sir," the butler replied. "Ah, fuck this," the sergeant muttered as he thundered out of the house and into the waiting taxi to take him to the *Ochan Arms*. There he drank ten of pints of watery ale before leading the invading forces of the Irish Army back to the docks to catch the ferry to Dublin carrying the news of the mission failure, stopping on the way to buy fifty fish and chip suppers.

Bumper Mc Sheehy and Martin Prendergast sat patiently all day waiting for a phone call with the good news, but the phone call never came! That night the pair were driven to the quays to await the arrival of the ferry where the dejected sergeant informed them Sir Bartley Dunne was absent from the island and on hearing this returned to the government offices to discuss strategy. "Boss, I'm sorry about this, we knew nothing about the governor being away for the summer it was bad luck and the plan was good." "Forget about it, Prendergast, we did our best and yes the plan was brilliant, but it wasn't meant to be. It's all over for us now, but at least we tried to do something." The ringing of the telephone interrupted him in mid-sentence. It was the British Prime Minister to inform the Irish Government, the cabinet had decided to suspend Stormont from midnight that night at which time a public announcement would be made of the immediate suspension of the Northern Ireland Government and the imposition of direct rule from London. Bumper Mc Sheehy slammed down the phone and leapt to his feet. "Jesus, Prendergast," he shouted, "I can't fuckin` believe it there is a God after all you probably got the gist of it, they're suspending Stormont. Jesus, this is fantastic news, Prendergast, it's a pity the Isle of Man adventure was a complete waste of time." "No, boss, no," the minister returned, "I have an idea, the communiqué we prepared for the surrender of the Isle of Man, we`ll change the wording and issue a statement immediately before the British make their announcement to the world's media." The revised communiqué read:

The government of the Irish Republic is pleased to announce that having given formal notice to the government of Northern Ireland of our intention to intervene militarily using the full might of the Irish Defence Forces including storm troopers from the elite unit of the Irish Army Rangers supported by auxiliary units of the FCA, the navy and Air Corp. to invade the occupied territories of the six counties of Ulster, the Stormont Government has capitulated to our military threat and we are pleased to inform the world direct rule from London will be announced tonight. The government wishes to pay tribute to the brave soldiers of the republic who trained incessantly for the past two days and were willing to work unsocial hours for the good of the nation.

Six weeks after the Horse O Houlihan mistakenly tried to force the butler to sign the papers transferring ownership of the Isle of Man to the Irish Government, Sir Bartley

25

Dunne and his wife returned to their mansion near Ochar where the butler related the incident to the governor. "But, who the hell was the damn fellow, if he was wearing an army uniform he must have been one of the actors making the film on the island." "I don't know, sir," the butler replied, "but he left these documents behind." Sir Bartley studied the papers closely. "Yes, of course, I know what these are, it`s that awful Manx language. Isn't there a crowd of bloody troublemakers down in Douglas trying to revive their stupid Manx that is nonsense, absolute nonsense? What is it with these Celtic people and their useless dead languages like the Irish and their bloody Gaelic had a run-in with that awful chap De Valera a few years ago, dreadful fellow, over the same bloody thing?" He tore up the document and threw it in the wastepaper basket. "Now, that's where that rubbish belongs. Yes, that was it; the whole incident was about the stupid Manx. The troublemakers were making a case for the revival of their silly language, will these people never learn?"

FAMILY REUNIONS

Detective or rather ex-detective, John Moran was glad to leave the hot crowded New York bar and clamber into the yellow cab awaiting him outside O Farrell`s Irish Pub on Seventeenth Avenue in downtown Manhattan. He smiled as he glanced back at his drunken ex-colleagues pouring onto the pavement shouting their goodbyes. "Where to buddy," the driver asked, "J.F.K," he responded. "Going on vacation, sir," the taxi driver inquired, "yeh, I suppose you could say that," he replied curtly in no humour for small talk. John Moran couldn't believe it, he was returning home after thirty-eight years, but why? If he was honest with himself, he wasn't sure. In all his time away, he had never given Ireland a second thought, but when he got the chance to retire from the N.Y.P.D. he took it; he was burnt out. All those years in the drug squad and all those years of drug abuse had taken their toll and, to the dismay of his friends and colleagues, he decided he was going home which they found strange as John Moran never mentioned Ireland. They knew he was Irish, or at least presumed so, but he didn't return on vacations and never spoke of his family. He was from a small village called Ballynaphuill in County Offaly, that's all he could recall, the name of the place. It was all a blank-as if his life in Ireland never existed, but why then was he in a taxi heading for the airport.

The girl at the Aer Lingus desk was surprised. "No luggage, sir." "No, hand luggage only," he replied, tightly clutching the holdall that contained all his worldly possessions, and checked the departure and arrival times. He had a good hour to spare and headed to the bar ordering a double brandy on the rocks, Hennessy his drink of choice; he liked the strong sweet taste, the fiery liquor giving him a warm glow from head to toe. On finishing his drink, he went to the gents, chose a cubicle, and opened his holdall, where carefully concealed in the lining was a bag of white powder. He neatly traced a line of cocaine on the cistern, snorting it through a rolled-up ten-dollar bill, waiting for the chemical rush." Christ," he muttered, "that stuff sure hit the spot." John Moran was a heavy drug user particularly of opioids not for the high, but to help him survive from day to day, erase the memories and dull the edge, easing the burden of the monkey on his back.

The story began when he`d been in the States less than a year and arrested as an illegal immigrant. He had no choice, military service in Vietnam in the pioneers attached to the marines or deportation to Ireland. On the flight to Saigon, a Mexican conscript told him. "Hombre Irlandes, my cousin Marcos is in the pioneers and he tells me they do all the dirty work for the marines, clean up dead bodies. And they force them to go down tunnels after the Viet Cong, and he says the tunnels are booby-trapped and full of snakes and poison gas, and none of the pioneers last long as a tunnel rat." These ominous words shook him to the core and as he sat in mute witness to the body bags laid row after row on the runway it was the final straw, he had to get out or die. He deserted, fled to Cambodia finding passage on a French ship bound for Canada and into the States, working as a barman in an Irish pub on the Eastside. Police officers of Irish descent frequented the bar and one of the regulars, Captain Sweeny from the Personnel Department, encouraged him to apply for a job in the N.Y.P.D. "Listen, son," he said, "the new administration is increasing the size of the force to tackle the growing crime in the city. Why don't you apply and I`ll make sure you get a position." "Captain Sweeny," he responded, "I`m illegal using a false identity and papers," not mentioning he was a deserter from the marines. The captain laughed. "Sure aren't half the Irish in the city illegal. It's not a problem at all; we can even use your real name if you like. We can change your date of birth and we`ll get you a new Social Security Number, the S.S.N. is the key to everything in the States, you`ll have a new identity and you can even apply for a passport. We Irish have to look out for each other, don't worry I`ll do the paperwork." Initially, he declined the captain's offer, however, changed his mind when the bar owner informed him officials were inquiring about the credentials of the bar staff and this worried him. Eventually, he`d be picked up and they would discover he was a deserter. He accepted Captain Sweeny`s offer on the basis that he might have a better chance of avoiding the marines if working in the N.Y.P.D. Two weeks later, to his utter astonishment, he received a letter in the name of John

Moran offering him a position as a junior detective in the drug squad and he hadn't even attended an interview, all down to the good Captain Sweeny. It was in the N.Y.P.D. he would spend the rest of his career; never marrying or forming close relationships aware the marines never, ever, gave up on deserters, always with that lingering fear of arrest irrespective of his new identity papers and job. Now that was all behind him, he was leaving the U.S.A. with a nice fat pension and a healthy bank account boosted by his dirty drug dealings. As the Aer Lingus Boeing departed J.F.K., he dozed off to be awoken from his twilight snooze by an airhostess shaking him gently. "Sir, wake up we`ve arrived in Dublin." It was snowing heavily as he stepped into the night and stood on home soil relishing the clean fresh air, and making his way through the crowded airport terminal hired a car at the Avis desk purchasing a map of Ireland. Leaving the airport, he followed a bus marked *City Centre* and on reaching the river Liffey, he would turn right and westward towards his destination. Twenty minutes later, however, he found himself driving through a bleak sprawling housing estate. *Christ, I must have followed the wrong fucking bus* and seeing a public house stopped to get directions and have a brandy or two. He entered *The Royal Oak Inn* and ordered a double brandy downing it in one greedy gulp, and ordering the same again asked the barman to show him on the map the route to Offaly. One of the customers, on hearing the American accent, approached him and introduced himself. "Hello, pal," he said in a direct friendly manner, "couldn't help hearing your accent; you're a Yank, right?" Moran nodded without speaking. "Can I buy yeh a drink, pal?" "Sure, buddy, sure," he replied. "Eddie Kelly's the name, now tell me what`s your poison." "I'll have a Hennessy, thank you, sir." "And what brings yeh to Finglas, pal?" "I was trying to find my way to Offaly and, well, I got kinda` lost," John Moran replied. "Offaly; Jesus, Mary, and Joseph," Eddie Kelly responded, "who the fuck in their right mind would want to go to awful bleedin` Offaly, now dat`s what I call a kip, awful bleedin` Offaly, nuthin` there but fuckin`bogs and more bogs and the odd sheep if you're unlucky." "That's where I'm from," Moran returned sharply, "I'm going home." "Ah, sorry now, pal," Eddie Kelly responded, aware his words had offended the man, "no offense intended, pal, only kiddin` so I was, lovely place Offaly, well if yeh like dat sort of thing. Wasn't I up there recently on a job, I'm an undertaker if yeh get me drift, bringing a body back to Dublin, a car crash it was. A travelling rug salesman from Stoneybatter, poor bastard killed outright when his car hit a sheep in the dark, awful mess, blood and guts everywhere, all over the bleedin` shop." "Listen, sir," John Moran replied dismissively, "it doesn't matter, to be honest, I can't even remember the place, I left home well over thirty years ago and ain`t ever been back." The undertaker was surprised. "What, pal, yeh mean yeh haven't seen your family or friends in over thirty years, and what about your parents are they still alive?" John Moran didn't reply and Eddie Kelly continued. "I was in Vietnam, can yeh believe that, pal, I was Ireland's sole representative in Uncle Sam's army, I was on Charlie`s bleedin`acre if yeh know what I mean, in the marines fightin` the Commies and you'll never believe what happened to me, a fuckin` amazing story. I've never

31

been Stateside, well not yet although me and the family are goin` over next summer to Detroit, it's where me mates live, Sonny and Jerome, ex-navy men. I even named me sons after them. Anyway, as I was sayin, ` pal, I was in the Nam but never been to the U.S.A.?" John Moran was puzzled and Eddie Kelly caught the look of disbelief. "Listen, pal, I'm not kiddin` yeh, ` here I've got a service medal to prove it." John Moran gazed at the triangle of red and yellow decoration with astonishment nearly choking on his drink. The word Vietnam brought it home to him, his thoughts interrupted when the undertaker inquired. "Did you serve in Vietnam, pal, and by the way I didn't get your name?" "John Moran, sir," came the swift reply. The undertaker stood speechless frozen on the spot. "Jesus, Mary, and Joseph, it couldn't be, no fuckin` way you're John Moran?" Much to Eddie Kelly's relief he replied. "Yes, sir, I`m John Moran, but never served in Vietnam, I was a police officer in New York and exempt from military service, never had the honour of serving my country, here." Opening his wallet, he flashed his warrant card. "Jasus," replied a thankful Edie Kelly, "for a moment there I thought you were someone else, he was called John Moran too. Now, he's someone I'd love to get me feckin` hands-on. I'd swing for dat bastard; he nearly got me killed in the Nam. I even have a bullet wound on me leg, shot by the slanty-eyed Charlie fuckers and all because of dat bastard John Moran. Christ, what a bloody coincidence you've got the same name —unbelievable." Through a drunken haze, Eddie Kelly fixed his keen gaze squarely on John Moran studying him closely. "Pal, are yeh sure now yeh were never in the Nam?" "No, sir, most definitely not," he replied, wondering what the hell the crazy undertaker was talking about. "And tell me, sir, what's this Moran guy got to do with you nearly getting killed in Vietnam?" Eddie Kelly was in his element, a chance to tell his story for the umpteenth time to anyone brave enough to listen. "Here, Pat," he shouted excitedly to the barman, "for fuck sake, give us the same again will yeh and a Hennessy for the Yank and make it a bleedin` double." John Moran stood silent captivated by the undertaker's story. Now it all made sense, why he was never picked up and all because of that asshole Sergeant Rock forcing Eddie Kelly into the marines in his name when he deserted. Christ, what an incredible story, of all the bars in the world he had to travel to Dublin, Ireland, and the chances of meeting this guy. "Jasus," Eddie said when he finished, "what a bleedin` coincidence, pal, what with you havin` the same fuckin` name, I just can't take it all in." With that, John Moran turned and shook Eddie's hand, leaving the bar to begin his two-hour drive. As he staggered home from *The Royal Oak Inn,* Eddie Kelly's mind raced. *Christ, what if the Yank had been the real John Moran, what would he have done then?* He couldn't wait to get home to tell his wife Collette, who was busy wrapping Christmas presents for Sonny and Jerome about the Yank he'd met in the pub.

The barman's directions were good and fifteen minutes later, he was driving towards County Offaly. *It was unbelievable, astonishing. After thirty-eight years, he was returning home and by pure chance in an out-of-town bar in the middle of nowhere, he meets the guy who*

33

took his place in the marines all those years ago and all because of Sergeant Rock who he remembered well – hard as nails. Yes, it was clear to him now, the reason he was never picked up, and all because of the undertaker Eddie Kelly. Nevertheless, Kelly was wrong to blame him for what happened; it was all down to Master Sergeant Rock. Through the darkness, he travelled along the empty road the swirling snowflakes casting a blanket of soft whiteness over the countryside. The silence punctuated by the weeping sound of the wiper blades sloshing back and forth when an almighty "***bang***" broke the trance, shattering the stillness of the night as the Ford Escort smashed into a low stone wall under the signpost stating Ballynaphuill, barely legible under a thin coat of frozen snow. "Jesus Christ," he screamed, wiping blood from his forehead with his sleeve, "that was a close shave I must have missed the fuckin` bend." He crawled out of the car into the cold night, dazed and lightheaded, head throbbing, blood running down his face. He was detached with no heaviness of body or aches or pains, barely able to walk, unable to touch the ground. He stumbled into the village, the windows of the small cottages illuminated by twinkling fairy lights, when before him stood the brightly lit pub *The Village Inn.* He knew he was home; they would all be inside, his family and neighbours, all gathered for Christmas Eve. He hesitated at the door listening to the sound of singing, laughing, and voices; voices he recognised. Yes, it was old hoary Fahy the schoolteacher, singing the same old rebel song; he listened intently. Yes, he smiled it was The Bold Fenian Men. *Christ, I thought Fahy would be dead by now he was an old man when I* *was a child*. Opening the door, he was assailed by a gush of warm turf-smelling air, hesitating momentarily before stepping into the bar. On entering the noisy room a hushed silence descended, all faces fixed on the stranger who invaded their private world in the middle of the dark midlands sixty miles from Dublin. "Double Hennessy," he ordered as the elderly barman stared keenly at his new customer. "Well, Holy God," he uttered, "I know you, your one of the Moran's from out Killymanish way aren't you, you're the image of your poor father. Sweet Jesus, your Charlie Moran's son, John, what the hell are you doing back here after all that happened?" The barman stood shaking his head as muffled whispers rose from the crowd all eyes on John Moran. "Same again", he barked, emptying the glass in one gulp. A hand touched his shoulder and turning was met with beautiful green tearful eyes. "John, why have you come back after all this time, you're not welcome here after all the pain and suffering you caused and your poor unfortunate parents, may God forgive you." John Moran stood transfixed by her harsh cutting words. "Why did you do it, John, why did you betray me with that half-wit over there and that thing, your living reflection in sin, the shame of it all?" As he gazed at the faded beauty standing before him, the long-lost memories came flooding back. Emir, his beloved Emir, Christ how could he have forgotten her, his first and only true love. "Emir, I'm sorry, I didn't mean to hurt you, how are you. It's so good to see you after all these years, my love." An angry voice halted the gentle conversation. "Come on, Emir, leave that bastard alone –good for nothing shite, come on let's go now we're going home." He recognised the voice; it was Dick Cooney his best friend from childhood. "Come on, Emir, leave that dirty fucker alone and you," he pointed his shaking finger at John Moran, "I don't know how you had the balls to show your face around here after what you did, you dirty lousy bastard." He stepped back shocked at the outburst. Emir was the love of his life, they were to be married, Dick was to be his best man, something terrible must have happened all those years ago, he should never have returned. He had to get away; everyone in the room was hostile giving him the evil eye, even the barman stood glaring at him. As he staggered towards the door, he heard a whisper, "John, John." The voice was familiar, and turning-faced two dishevelled figures huddled together in a dark corner of the snug; so old, so pitiful, so helpless. He peered into the semi-darkness and stepped back in shock, confronting him was his mother and father. "Mammy, Daddy," he cried. His father stopped him. "John, you're not welcome here, you shouldn't have come back." He glanced at the shrunken figures of his parents and wheeled around towards the door, but as he grasped the handle, a laughing voice called. "Johnny Boy, Johnny Boy, any chance of the ride tonight, any chance of a roll in the hay like the old times." He looked at his mocker, a drunken obese woman sitting in the corner. "Do you not remember me, Johnny Boy, you and me rolling in the hay?" She laughed again, and he noticed beside her the awkward figure sipping Guinness through a straw, a man in a child's body staring back at him. "I called him after you, Johnny Boy; he's your spitting` image now, isn't he?" The figures laughed. "Daddy, Daddy," the child-man uttered as John Moran reeled back shuddering, gasping for breath.

It was a summer day thirty-eight years ago and he was cutting hay, shirtless in the sweltering heat up in the big field, and Brigit Flynn one of his neighbour's children, stood at the gate staring at him as he toiled under the blistering sun, a simple but harmless girl. Although only fourteen he couldn't help notice how well developed she was, her ample breasts heaving through her skimpy cotton summer dress and the way she stood gazing at him. He went to the barn to sharpen the scythe, and when looking for the whetstone came upon a bottle of his father's poteen taking a couple of long deep swigs, the pungent drink making him lightheaded. And there she was standing at the barn door, all innocent, smiling at him and closing the door behind her came close to him, so close he felt the warmth of her breasts against his naked chest and the look in her eye. His body quivered with excitement the blood rushing to his head; he couldn't help himself pushing her roughly on the straw bedding. She screamed hysterically. "Johnny Boy, stop it, stop it, you're hurting me." However, Johnny Boy couldn't stop and overcome with animal passion violently raped her. When lust expended he lay back, body covered in sweat and straw, staring blankly at the roof ashamed to look at Brigit Flynn who lay weeping and, as if awakened from her nightmare, leaped to her feet and ran out, clothes in shreds, blood running down her legs. He had to go, to get away and escape, it was all over in Ballynaphuill for John Moran, and a fortnight later, he was in the U.S.A.

In the early hours of a Christmas morning, Sergeant Mulligan drove into the small village nearly missing the abandoned car that sat askew, its shimmering headlights barely visible through the soft flurry of snow. Parking behind the Ford Escort with the Dublin number plates, he shook his sleeping colleague. "Dignam, wake up for fuck sake looks like a crash, come on now sleepy head the fierce cold will soon wake yeh up." The doors were locked, and Sergeant Mulligan wiped a layer of snow off the side window —no sign of life. He shone his torch into the car where slumped over the steering wheel was the lifeless body of a man, empty brandy bottle in hand, bulky form silhouetted in the torchlight. "Jesus, Dignam, there a body in the car, smash the glass with your baton and open the door." As the glass shattered, they were met with the stink of alcohol and sweat. "Christ, it smells like a bloody brewery in here, he's dead, Dignam, dead as a feckin`doornail, he must have lost control of the car on the bend; it's happened a couple of times before, Jesus, look at the blood on the windscreen. Yeh better call the hospital in Tullamore and get an ambulance over here to remove the body, there's nothing we can do for this gentleman, whoever he is?" As they waited for the ambulance, Garda Dignam searched the car and handed Sergeant Mulligan the holdall. "Here, serge, it was under the body."On opening the bag, he discovered a wrap of white powder, a roll of dollar bills, and a U.S. passport that he opened looking closely at the name. "Christ," he shouted, "it can't be, not after all this time, I don't believe it, and that's where he's been hiding all these years." "Do you know him, serge?" "Yes, I do, Dignam; he left

Ballynaphuill just after I started on the force. Christ, it was shocking, so it was." "What happened, serge?" "Well, it was my first big case, your man there got drunk on poteen and raped a mentally retarded girl, you know her now, Dignam, Brigit Flynn, the one with the disabled son." "Jesus, serge, is this fella the father?" "Yes, he is or should I say was, but why did he come back especially after what happened to his poor parents." "What happened to his parents?" "Well," the sergeant replied, "after he raped the girl he ran away and a warrant issued for his arrest but we never found him and that's what I can't fathom why he came back after thirty-plus years?" "But, tell me about the parent's, serge?" "Well, as you know the Flynn girl gave birth to a handicapped boy he's called Johnny, harmless lad all the same." "For fuck sake, serge, will yeh ever tell me what happened to the parents?" "Well, Dignam, they were shunned by their neighbours for the awful crime their son, who was their only child, had committed. The locals called the Flynn boy, Moran`s Moran, and the shame of it became too much for the couple, so they became recluses seldom leaving their farm. Anyway, many years later one-market day old Charlie Moran, John's father, came to town to sell cattle and went into *The Village Inn* for a few pints. There he is sitting alone in the snug, ignored by the punters, when Lord above doesn't Brigit Flynn and her son who was now in his teens and the spitting image of his father come into the bar. Jesus, it was a remarkable sight to behold, Dignam. She`d buy her son a pint of Guinness but he couldn't hold the glass, so the young fella Flynn would sip the Guinness through a straw. Jasus doesn't Brigit say something to old Charlie which upset him, to put it mildly. So, he goes home grabs his shotgun and shoots Missus Moran, blows her head clean off, and then hangs himself in the barn he just couldn't live with the shame. Talk about paying for your family's sins, Christ it was awful, Dignam, I still have nightmares about the terrible scene, I think the sight of young Johnny Flynn drove him over the edge, imagine having to live in a close-knit community like Ballynaphuill, Jesus it must have been absolute hell for poor Charlie and his wife." Garda Dignam stood speechless as he gazed at the crumpled heap that was John Moran. *Christ, why he came back after all the hurt he had caused, and his unfortunate parents. And when he does return he's full of drink and drugs and kills himself, but at least he never knew the terrible fate that befell his poor mother and father or about his son!* Sergeant Mulligan broke the silence. "Dignam," he ordered, "radio the barracks and get a tow truck to take the car away before anyone sees it, then radio Saint Mary's Hospital and get them to call that Dublin undertaker, what do yeh call him now, the fella who went on and on about Vietnam. He worked with us last year when he removed the body of the salesman killed in the car crash at Kinnitty. Eddie Kelly, that's the name, ask them to get him here tonight and take the body up to Glasnevin for burial, I`ll do the paperwork. We don't want to upset anyone around here especially the Flynn`s. Nobody needs to know John Moran came home except the undertaker Kelly and us. And make sure he gets a Christian burial, even Moran deserves that." "Okay, I`m on the case, serge, but tell me something now. Why do you think John

Moran came back after all these years?" "Well, Dignam, I`m not sure, but there's an old saying and it goes like this. *Irish people always like to keep one foot in the place they were born,* so I suppose you could say he came home to die. Jesus, Dignam, a tragic case indeed."

Note *This short story was originally written as a finale to my novel `**The Undertakers Assistant**` in which Eddie Kelly, an undertaker from Dublin, becomes an accidental stowaway on a U.S. warship bound for Vietnam where he is forced into the Marine Corp. to take the place of the deserter, John Moran.*

UP IN SMOKE

The Town, 1971

Majella loved Mickey and he loved her. Childhood sweethearts, engaged at sixteen and married at eighteen. To Majella, he was her strong handsome man who would protect and love her, always. To Mickey, she was his beautiful sexy woman who would care for and love him, always. Before they married, the couple decided to purchase a small, two-up, two-down, terraced house near the town centre that was affordable and within walking distance of where they worked. Mickey in the Social Services Department and Majella in the local pharmacy. However, there was a serious drawback; the house was without heating, bathroom, or hot water and Majella`s mother shook her head in disbelief when she viewed the property. "Jesus, Mary, and Joseph," she exclaimed, "this place is a feckin` kip." Moreover, when she saw the brick-built, whitewashed, lean-to, outside toilet she was appalled. "Are you two bloody mad or what, you can't live in this dump it should be knocked down, you're moving in with me? There's plenty of room in my house and you know you're more than welcome?" However, the couple rejected the kind offer and proceeded with the purchase as they dearly wished to set up home together, and there was another factor. The town council had introduced a grant scheme to address the widespread problem of substandard housing and offered financial aid towards the cost of renovations. Accordingly, the couple became the proud owners of a rundown, two-up, two-down, red brick-built Edwardian dwelling house on the sloped cul-de-sac of twelve neat and orderly terraced houses without gardens. As the council only contributed fifty per cent of the building costs, they had to raise a considerable amount of money before they could renovate and build their rear, two-story, bathroom over kitchen extension. Every morning Mickey jumped out of bed at half-past seven, rushing down the stairs to light the four rings on the gas cooker to heat the scullery and filled a large saucepan and kettle with water that he placed on the cooker to boil. As he sat on the toilet inhaling his first cigarette contemplating the day ahead, she would shout. "Mickey, how long does it take you to go to the toilet, if yeh don't hurry up I'll wet myself." While Majella used the toilet, he would make two cups of instant coffee, two slices of toast, and fill a large plastic basin with hot water, which he placed on the living room table. As she stood washing her slim lithe body with a facecloth and soap, he'd stand in the scullery shaving, a small mirror in one hand, razor in the other. "Don't be gawking now, Mickey, and don't be getting any funny ideas either, I know what you're like." Majella was extremely modest, even in front of her husband, and he would stand with his back to her carefully adjusting the mirror to enjoy his wife's pert bosom and supple curves. He had been late for work a few mornings when his youthful passion and compelling desire overcame him and rushing into the living room, he would embrace her passionately and make mad love on the cold bare floorboards. "You're going to get it now, spit on me beautiful," he`d shout, "I`m cumin` with the mighty mallet to give it to you hard and fast, get up the yard Missus C." "No, Mickey, not now," she`d protest laughingly, "I've just washed and I`ll be late for work again." Every night, fire piled high with coal as the couple sat huddled together, overcoats on or wrapped in blankets, watching television and Mickey questioned himself as to the wisdom of purchasing the property. *Jesus Christ, the sooner I get started the better, it would freeze the balls off a brass monkey in this place, I only hope Majella can stick it out until the work`s complete.* However, despite these initial difficulties Majella was excited about the prospect of the extension and decided to fit the bathroom with the new coloured plastic suites in Jade Green or Turquoise Blue she'd seen in the *House and Home* magazine at the hairdressers one Saturday. They looked forward to starting a family, however, this important event had to be postponed until they had heating and bathroom facilities; so saving the required cash of paramount importance. When they moved in Mickey, with the help of his best friend and work colleague Donal, painstakingly stripped off the existing flowery, wartime flock wallpaper. Then they papered the complete interior with the new-fangled woodchip that was great for hiding the lumps and bumps associated with wall plaster in old houses managing to transform the dreary interior with the application of a matt finish magnolia emulsion, introducing a modern feel with the inviting smell of fresh paint. Even Majella`s mother was impressed. "Not bad," she said, "a big improvement if I do say so myself."

They were the youngest residents on the street and initially encountered hostility because they came from the new estate. However, Majella's natural charm and Mickey's open friendliness overcame these issues. Their popularity grew when Majella collected prescriptions and delivered medicines and Mickey always at hand to assist with odd jobs and sort out any concerns. Every night one of the neighbours would knock on the door. "Mickey, son, I`m having a problem with me pension, can you help me?" and he would always reply. "Of course I can, my pleasure, delighted to be of assistance." Over time, the tight-knit community came to accept Mickey and Majella with the exception of a man in his late sixties called Sammy Ogle, who was disdainful and openly antagonistic. "Never trust anyone from the new estate," he would tell his neighbours, "you know what that crowd is like, they just can't be trusted." While everything was fine at first a problem developed in their marriage. It wasn't that they had fallen out of love or that he (or she) had met someone else. No, it was none of the aforementioned issues, often the source of marital difficulties, in their case it was something different! To put it simply, Majella was the cause as she suffered from an inherent genetic defect passed on from mother to daughter and most likely from generation to generation. It was a serious issue and endemic in the town, causing considerable strain on their relationship and taking all of his patience at times not to walk away. And, what was this all-encompassing problem? It was simple- nagging! Majella had become a prolific nagger, nagging Mickey incessantly, never stopping except to draw breath. She nagged him about everything, rambling on and on about the delay in getting the house refurbished, his two nights a week at the martial arts club, his Friday night drinking, and endlessly about his smoking habit. Her father, Joe had died the previous year from a smoking-related illness and she never stopped reminding him, and strangely, the more she nagged about smoking the more he smoked. Mickey`s pet name for his wife was *Saint Majella of the Worriers* as he figured out that the cause of nagging was worry, plain and simple. He knew the town was full of natural-born worriers and consequently full of natural-born naggers.

One night, at his martial art class, his trainer Sean O Kane called him into the office. "Mickey, there's a new nightclub opening next week and the owner Ken Gunne is looking for bouncers, do you fancy a job. I've taken up the offer and starting on Friday night as head of security. Mickey wasn't interested; in the first instance, his wife wouldn't let him. She hated him out of the house at night also he didn't fancy dealing with every drunk in the town and the town was full of drunks. "No thanks, Sean, while the few extra quid would be useful I couldn't take the grief I`d get from the missus." "Okay, Mickey, but the job`s open for you anytime if you change your mind." The following Friday after work, Mickey went as usual to the Palace Bar for a few pints with his work colleagues Donal Devine and Peter Cavanagh, however, he got bored with Peter, their trade union official, going on persistently about a legal claim the union was taking against the department. "Listen, guys," Peter said, "we can win this case, I'm confident about that and there`s a lot of back pay involved, a small fortune." He kept going on about the pay grades for a similar job being higher on the mainland and they demanded parity of esteem. Finally, Mickey could take no more trade union talk and making his excuses left the crowded bar. On his way home he called at the Chinese restaurant, as he did every Friday night, and ordered special fried rice, sweet and sour chicken, and gravy chips. Next, the off-license where he purchased a bottle of Riesling sweet German wine for Majella and a dozen cans of Harp lager and twenty Sweet Afton cigarettes for himself. It was after the meal when he lit a cigarette the nagging commenced. "Mickey," she said in a low monotonous voice, "why do you have to smoke, look what happened to my poor father but you don't care, do you? Kill yourself and leave me here on my own, selfish that's what you are. I can't go on living like this and what about the house. I feel dirty all the time and the money you spend on cigarettes. Why did we buy this kip, I can`t believe you brought me to live here; my mother was right about you she thinks you're the village idiot out for a walk. Yes, that's what she thinks about you bringing me to this dump." Finally, he had enough and without responding stormed out of the house racing down the hill to his part-time job as a bouncer in the new club to escape his nagging wife and save their marriage.

While his role as a bouncer allowed him to earn extra money it had other benefits such as free drinks after closing and the odd drunk female (normally divorced) in an amorous mood seeking male company which he always declined. However, after a few months, the initial novelty wore off. Despite the nagging he disliked leaving Majella alone and he disliked working into the early hours, so he decided to inform Sean he was leaving, however, an event occurred which changed his mind. One night he noticed the fire escape door ajar and as he shut it, smelt the unmistakable pungent aroma of cannabis. There were two of them, two young lads giggling uncontrollably unaware of his presence. "Okay, you two," he barked, "the games up, now hand over the gear or I'm calling the cops." "Mickey, take the dope just don't get the cops involved I could lose me job, it'll never happen again we promise you." They handed him a couple of ready-rolled joints and he escorted them to the door. "Now, fuck off you two you're barred, and don't ever show your faces here again," he shouted as the pair, laughing hysterically, zigzagged across the road. Mickey was not a dope smoker as he had a bad experience with cannabis when he was at the college. His classmate, Shorty Scully managed to get his hands on cannabis resin and Mickey and his friends went to the park and smoked the dope accompanied by copious amounts of Buckfast tonic wine. He was violently ill and confined to his bed for two days unsure if it was the dope or the wine that made him sick. In any case, he was wary of smoking dope but his best mate Donal wasn't, and he intended to give him the joints the following day. When he got home, Majella was in bed so he opened a can of Harp lager intending to watch a video. But, panic stations he couldn't find his cigarettes, and as he frantically rummaged through his pockets came to the shocking realisation he must have left them on the bar counter, what would he do? He was devastated, the club was closed, Jesus, where at this late hour would he get cigarettes, it was imperative he got cigarettes. He remembered the confiscated joints; having a smoke was crucial and in desperation would smoke anything to satisfy his craving and lifting the scuttle threw coal on the fire as he sat back to watch a film on his new Betamax video player that he'd rashly bought the purchase of which caused him untold grief with Majella. He lit the joint inhaling deeply and by the time he smoked the second he was wasted, flying high and euphoric as he slumped back on the couch giggling to himself. *So, it wasn't the cannabis that made me sick the first time I tried it; it must have been the two bottles of Bucky wine I necked down!* Beginning that fateful night, happy and high, Mickey Coyle slowly and surely began his short journey to becoming a dedicated dope fiend. He came to love his Friday and Saturday nights –his cannabis nights. He would scour the club for anyone smoking dope and confiscate their gear. He was only doing his job and this was a perk ensuring a constant supply of free cannabis. However, a couple of joints over the weekend developed into a sneaky joint or two during the week. He loved his dope; it was the best thing in his life after Majella of course and the perfect panacea for his wife`s nagging. When he clambered into bed after his long shift she`d begin in the same low droning voice. "Mickey, what time of the night is this to be coming home. I hope you're not up to any funny business at the club. I've heard rumours about the dirty sex goings-on in that place with the married men and women and their swinger`s parties and by the way you smell like a brewery, and what's that awful pong, your clothes and hair smell like an ashtray." She`d ramble on and on and he would lie in the darkness counting cracks on the ceiling, smiling to himself as he drifted into an ocean of tranquillity her voice fading into the distance. It was what he enjoyed most about smoking dope, the intoxicating sleep far from the incessant prattling of his wife.

Now, the town was a small place with a small number of dope smokers who soon caught on to the fact that Mickey the bouncer was a dope fiend, freeloader, and using his position to fleece them of their precious cannabis. Accordingly, they stopped frequenting the club or at least stopped carrying or smoking dope on the premises. One night after a long period of forced abstinence, he smelt it, someone was smoking dope in the club, and instinctively his nose took him to the offenders-a young couple sitting in semi-darkness. As he approached, the young man stubbed out the joint. "Ah, Mickey, give us a break, I'm back at university tomorrow, please don't bar us." He knew the young man, Paddy Carlin whose family lived beside Majella`s mother and was studying horticulture in England. "Okay, Paddy, you and your girlfriend can stay," he said, "but only on one condition, you give me enough gear for a few spliffs, and by the way what sort of dope is it, it smells strong, where did you buy it?" "Mickey, I didn't buy it, I grow the gear at my pad in Liverpool, its home-grown grass called Purple Haze it`s brilliant gear.

Here, it`s all I have left," he said, handing him a small plastic bag, "enough for a few joints, enjoy." "Exactly what I intend to do Paddy." When he got home he tore open the bag that contained a leafy green substance with a powerful odour, grass, he'd never smoked grass before. After a couple of puffs, his head spun. *Wow, this is good gear and much more potent than the usual Lebanese Gold* he muttered as he sprawled out on the sofa mind racing, a grin as wide as the ocean across his face. The next morning he went to Donal's house where he lived with his mother and his brother Charlie who was a bit of a tearaway. Donal`s father Albert a retired florist having died a few years previous. "Donal, I caught your man Paddy Carlin smoking grass last night and I tried some, brilliant gear and it sure gave me the wibbly wobblies all right, fuckin` stoned out of me head so I was, the best gear I've ever smoked. It's called Purple Haze and you'll never believe it, it`s home-grown. Your man fuckin`Carlin grows his own weed." Donal was fascinated at the prospect of growing quality grass, what a challenge and what rewards. His father taught him the basics and a bonus was their large greenhouse although dilapidated as Charlie had smashed the glass. "Mickey," he said, "I've got a brilliant idea, why don't we fix up the greenhouse and grow our own weed? We`ll have a ready supply and here's the good bit, we can sell the rest and make a fortune; you'll have the cash to renovate the house for Majella in no time." Mickey's face lit up and he threw his arms around his friend. "Donal, you little beauty, me best mucker, what a brilliant plan." "Mickey, we`ll have to speak to Paddy Carlin and get the know-how for the job.

See if you can get his phone number and we can give him a shout if he can grow the gear, so can we. On the way home Mickey stopped at his local pub Magill`s for a pint or two. "Here, Billy," he shouted to the barman, "give us a pint of plain will yeh." As he sat sipping the stout, he ran Donal's plan through his mind. *If they could grow gear like Carlins, it would be fantastic. Donal had green fingers and they had the glasshouse, but what excited him was selling the gear. He could use his position in the club to shift the grass and make a big pile of cash in a short time. He knew all the dope heads and if caught he'd say he confiscated the gear off the punters. He could start the extension and refurbish the house making Majella`s dreams come true-brilliant, now we`re laughing. He could see it now, every morning before work him and Majella in the steamy hot shower- lathering her sexy body in a rich, bubbly, foamy, frothy soap –Jesus, stop the lights, beam me up Scottie- down boy, down!* "Hey, Billy," he shouted excitedly, "the same again and have one yourself." "You're in great form today, Mickey, did yeh have an 18/1 win on the horses or what?" "No, much better than that, Billy, much better indeed," he replied blushing slightly. The following night he called to a town centre bar *The Anchor* where he knew Carlin`s brother worked. "Dermot, I'm trying to contact Paddy, he applied for a part-time job in the club over the summer holidays and Ken Gunne was looking for his contact details, do yeh have them?" "Yeh, sure, Mickey," he replied, handing him a piece of paper with the phone number. Mickey rang Paddy Carlin who told him there was a specialist shop on the London Road in Liverpool called *The Indoor*

Gardening Centre that sold all the necessary paraphernalia to grow cannabis. Planning their new venture they soon realised the main obstacle was cash or more correctly, lack of cash. "Mickey," said Donal despondently, "where the hell are we going to get our hands on five hundred pounds if not more, we might as well give up the ghost?" Mickey stood silent for a few moments. "I can get the money," he said with a hint of reluctance, "we can use the money I've saved for the house; I have about six hundred pounds in the Credit Union and that should be more than enough to get things moving." Donal was shocked. "Mickey, we can't touch your saving are you crazy or what, Majella would go mad." "It'll be worth it, Donal, I can start the extension sooner than later and she need never know a thing, the savings account is in my name. I can temporarily withdraw the money and she'll be none the wiser."

So, the cannabis operation commenced; saving's withdrawn, broken glass replaced, and hiring a car they boarded the ferry to Liverpool, the date chosen coinciding with a cup final between Liverpool and Everton and Liverpool being Mickey's team giving them the perfect alibi. Paddy Carlin taught them the basics and they returned with the requisite knowledge and equipment. Donal was meticulous: every procedure considered in minute detail: heat: moisture: temperature, water, and humidity-nothing overlooked; they would grow the perfect cannabis plants —yes, they would! The weeks passed, the seeds germinated, and the fledgling plants blossomed under their loving care. However, of the seeds planted, only twelve germinated, and these plants Mickey proudly called *The Twelve Apostles* each plant christened with an apostle's name. Peter, Thomas, Matthew, James, Judas, and so on, and at work, they would openly discuss the development of each plant. "How's Peter today?" Mickey would inquire. "Fine, solid as a rock, Donal, although I have my doubts about young Thomas. James the Greater is doing great, but less so James the Lesser, and Judas looks suspect to me. Also, I find Matthew a bit fishy and that Andrew fella very taxing." They painstakingly cared for their plants and *The Twelve Apostles* matured and blossomed until only two weeks remained before they could harvest their valuable crop and enjoy the fruits of their devoted labours when their luck changed for the worse. One morning Donal arrived at work in a terrible state. "Mickey, I`ve got bad news, very bad news, it's about the plants." "What's wrong, Donal, what's the matter?" "Mickey," he replied, "It`s like this, Peters went bald, Thomas has a short back and sides, James the Great is not great anymore, James the Lesser is even lesser and...," he continued, "poor Judas has been plucked to death, Matthew has been scalped and I forgot to mention poor Andrew, he's now a skinhead." "What the hell are you on about, Donal, what's happened to the plants?" "Mickey, you have to see for yourself, we`ll go over during the lunch break."At twelve-thirty, they charged across town and Mickey stood flummoxed and speechless; most of the plants were stripped of their exuberant lush green vegetation and stood gaunt and bare. "What the fuck happened, Donal, who did this?" "Mickey, I'm sorry it was Charlie and his mates when they came in from the pub last night they stupidly stripped most of the plants for the gear but hey mucker it's not all bad. I reckon three of the plants are salvageable all we need is a couple of weeks, however, you'll have to take them to your house they won't last long here, either we move them or lose them if we sell the gear we can at least get some of your money back?" "And tell me now what good is that," Mickey returned angrily, "back to square one after all the hard work. I blame you for not controlling that brother of yours; you're too lackadaisical." "Mickey, I`m sorry but we have to get them out of here pronto, we`ve got to take them to your house right now." "Jesus, Donal, are you fuckin` mad or what if Majella finds out about us growing dope and losing the money my marriage is over, I couldn't risk it no fuckin`way, not in a million years." "Hold on a second, Mickey, I know how we can handle it and Majella need never know what the plants are. Listen, my father, God rest his soul, used to place plastic flowers and tomatoes on bare plants to make them appear to be blooming or bearing fruit he told me it was a trick of the trade, hold on a second." He rummaged through a pile of old cardboard boxes and found what he was looking for. "Here," he said, handing Mickey a box of small red plastic tomatoes, "we`ll stick them on the branches and they'll look like real tomato plants, you can tell Majella your growing tomatoes and she`ll never know the difference. Put one plant in the living room and one in each of the bedroom windows." Nevertheless, Mickey was not convinced; Majella wasn't stupid although she knew nothing about plants, however this way he could at least get some of his money back. From a distance, they did look similar to tomato plants; yes, the plan could work. "Right, Donal, I`m taking the plants now and tell that brother of yours he's a dead man when I get my fuckin` hands on him."

When Majella arrived home, she noticed the plant festooned with plastic tomatoes. "Mickey, what`s a tomato plant doing in the window?" "Ah, Donal`s growing a load of them and he gave me a couple, I always liked tomatoes," he replied confidently. Everything was fine for a week until Majella commented. "Jesus, Mickey, I woke up during the night, I was having a terrible nightmare about the B Specials coming into the bedroom and shooting me, it was as if I was on drugs and the smell coming from the plants was overpowering." Mickey squirmed. "Not to worry, darling, it's the fertiliser it has a strong smell, I'll ask Donal to come over when he gets a chance and take them." "Mickey, they're ready," Donal proclaimed on examining the plants Friday lunchtime. Mickey was ecstatic the risk paid off. After work in the club, he would harvest and bag them for selling the next night. When he arrived home, he stopped dead in his tracks-the living room light was on which was unusual. After their Friday night Chinese meal and a few glasses of white wine, Majella would watch the Late Late Show on R.T.E. and be in bed by ten-thirty to be up early to go shopping with her best friend Imelda. Something was wrong he knew this instinctively, and entering the house full of trepidation found his wife crying hysterically and on seeing him, she flew into a rage. "Mickey, how could you do this to me?" "What`s the matter, Majella, for God's sake what`s happened?" "You know fine well what the matter is, did you take me for a fool. Tomato plants my arse; I know what your little game is. When Sammy Ogle was passing, he knocked on the window and when I opened the door, he asked me what the plant was and when I stupidly replied. It's a tomato plant, Sammy, Mickey's growing them he laughed and said." "Majella, tell that husband of yours tomatoes plants don't grow in the winter. I hope you two are not up to any funny business, I know what you crowd from the new estate are like, if it`s anything illegal I'll have to report you, I'm an ex- B Special you know." "I was mortified, Mickey, of all the people in the street it had to be Sammy Ogle, it`s drugs isn't it; I knew you and Donal were up to something." Without waiting for his response, she grabbed her coat, rushed towards the front door, and turning said. "Mickey, I'm leaving, I'm getting a taxi up to my mother's house and I'll be back first thing in the morning for my things, how could you. I'll never forgive you for this and by the way, I'm calling at the police station to report you and your drugs, you'll go to jail and see if I care." She slammed the door and stormed down the street. *Jesus, how could I have been so stupid, if that bastard Charlie hadn't messed with the plants this would never have happened and that bloody old fool Sammy Ogle, nosey little fucker interfering in my business, he'd make the bastard pay and he knew Ogles dirty little secrets, oh yes he did.*

Late one Friday night he heard the sound of rollicking laughter and loud bawdy shouts coming from the last house in the cul-de-sac Sammy Ogle`s, and peeking through a clink in the dusty Venetian blinds was confronted by an astounding hullaballoo. The living room was crowded with all the local fogies, all ex-special constables, a couple of A Specials, three or four B Specials, a handful of C Specials, and one D Special. On the far wall, a white sheet hung where flickering black and white images of naked women in various obscene poses danced wildly across the screen and he could just make out the barely legible title *Lady Godiva* and there he was, drooling Sammy Ogle operating the projector, manic grin on face, pint bottle of Smithwick`s ale in hand. The old men were watching dirty films and drinking, shouting obscenities to the background of loud ribald laughter.

He grabbed a can of Harp from the fridge, sat back heavily, and lighting a cigarette pondered the situation. *No, Majella would never go to the police, no, that would never happen. He`d blame Donal for everything, but in the first instance, he had to harvest the plants.* Working feverishly, he cut and bagged two plants stopping when he heard a noise outside. It was a vehicle reversing up the hill and running over to the window parted a small section of the curtain, his heart skipped a beat: his worst nightmare. A police Land Rover parked outside its engine purring softly, a figure dismounted and walked towards the door. *The bitch, she's gone and squealed to the peelers.* The horror of the situation flashed before him. *His family would be disgraced in the town; he'd lose his wife, house, and job even his government pension, and spend* *countless years in jail all because of a few bloody cannabis plants, Christ, how he could have been so fucking stupid.* He stood frozen, pumping adrenalin, sweat covering his trembling body as he waited for the crash- bang of his front door smashing in and the house full of peelers -but nothing, he composed himself. Maybe they're awaiting the army, or sniffer dogs or whatever, so he decided he wasn't going down without a fight. A chair was placed stoutly against the front door; the bags of grass thrown on the fire, but heavily saturated with resin the grass hissed billowing grey smoke, so he sprinkled lighter fuel on the smouldering heap which ignited flames roaring up the chimney. Frantically he shoved the uncut plant into the burning mass until nothing remained but a heap of grey ash and a smoke-filled room, expecting the door to burst open to the shouts of *Drug Squad- Drug Squad, It's a Bust- It's a Bust,* but they never came. He crept into the front hall, removed the chair, and gently lifted the letterbox to be greeted by the posterior of a policeman standing in his doorway. On hearing the letterbox open, the surprised policeman bent down looking Mickey directly in the eye, and said apologetically. "Sorry for disturbing you, sir, pulled into the street for a ciggie, your cul-de-sac is handy for a bit of privacy away from the prying eye of the inspector, we`ll be on our way now, sir, goodnight to you." As he walked towards the Land Rover he stopped, turned, and tapped gently on the door. Mickey, who stood in a trance jumped back, bent down, and opened the letterbox to be confronted by the policeman peering back at him who inquired in a soft voice. "Sir, is there something burning, there's an awful smell emanating from your house, the whole street stinks is everything alright?" "It`s nothing, officer," he replied brazenly, "I fell asleep and burned the chip pan, the wife's away for the night, but it`s all under control now, nothing for you to worry about, thank you." When the Land Rover departed, he sat in darkness his body lathered in sweat, and as he sipped a cold beer tears filled his eyes. *Christ, what a bloody mess, everything up in smoke, and further away from the extension than ever and he'd have to tell Majella about their saving and she`d leave him, but at least she hadn't squealed to the cops and he wasn't going to jail.* Majella arrived early the next morning. "Jesus, Mickey, what's that awful smell." "I burned the plants, everything you said was right I was a fool, it was all Donal`s fault." "Yes, I know," she replied, "I met him last night on the way to town and he told me how he sweet-talked you into taking the plants." "Did he now, at least he`d the decency to own up. Here, Majella, give us a hug, you're the apple of my eye and I'm sorry about everything, I love you so much you know that don't you." "Yes, of course," she replied. "Majella, tell me, darling, would you have squealed to the cops?" "Well, to tell the truth, Mickey, I was angry with you last night, I wasn't thinking straight and on my way to the police station I met Donal, and when he took the blame I calmed down and he persuaded me not to report the drugs. Nevertheless, it hasn't changed anything, I'm not stopping I only came back for my clothes, I`m moving into my mother's house until you get everything sorted, that caper with the drugs was the last straw. I'm not coming back until the house is finished." Mickey sat staring into the pile of cold grey embers as his wife walked out without saying goodbye. *How could he have been so thoughtless expecting her to live in squalor in a house without heat or bathroom? She was right, he was selfish, why couldn't he have rented a decent flat in the town for a couple of years until they saved a deposit for a proper house, yes, he was a selfish bull-headed fool?* Loud banging on the door interrupted his thoughts-it was Donal. "Mickey, I'm sorry about all this, I know Majella`s walked out I met her last night, Jesus you'd a lucky escape she was heading to the cop shop to report you. I can't believe it, thank God I ran into her or you`d be fucked, what about the plants where are they?" "Donal, I burned them last night, a cop car came up the street and I panicked, I thought Majella had shopped me, but the cops were only stopping for a cigarette." "Christ, Mickey, you mean everything gone; it was all a waste of time." "Yeh, Donal, a waste of your time and my fuckin` money and I hope you didn't mention the savings to Majella." "No, Mickey, I didn't do you think I'm stupid or what, anyway, what are we going to do?" "I'll tell you exactly what you're going to do, fuck face, buy me a few pints in Magill's, I need a drink, let`s go."

Mickey`s life was a disconsolate mess without his wife, wandering between work, the pub, and bed. On Wednesday lunchtime, he called around to her workplace. "Majella, I miss you so much, please come home." "Mickey, I miss you too but I`m not going back until you get the house finished, listen, why don't you come up and stay in my mother's house." His heart skipped a beat and for a fleeting moment considered doing just that, but he knew he couldn't, it would be admitting defeat and his mother–in–law would gloat and wallow in the shame of his failure. No, he was staying put until things were sorted, one way, or another! On Friday night, a week after his close encounter with the law he returned home, sitting in darkness, fire unlit, watching a video Sean lent him. Then the same occurrence as the previous week, a police Land Rover reversing up the street and stopping outside except now he`d nothing to hide. He opened the front door and the same policeman stood smoking. "Hello again, sir, hope we haven't disturbed you now." "No, officer, not at all but can you help me with something." "Certainly, sir, do have you a problem?" "Officer, can you tell me is it an offence to have pornographic films and show them to members of the public." "Yes, sir, I can confirm that it is indeed an offence under *The Obscenities Order 1950.*" The constable expressed interest. "Why, sir, have you something to report to the police?" "I have officer, right here on this street, right under your nose, follow me and I'll show you the house, it`s the end of the terrace." It was the usual Friday night old boy's porn party and Sammy Ogle, on opening the door mouth dribbling, dropped his bottle of Smithwicks. "Officer, what's the problem, I'm an ex-special constable, we`re all ex-special constables, it's our Friday night weekly reunion. "Sir," the policeman declared officiously, "we have reason to believe you have in your possession pornographic material in contravention of *The Obscenities Order 1950*, we`re seizing the offensive material and arresting you and your co-offenders to appear before the magistrate in the morning can you follow me, sir?" As Ogle and his companions clambered into the back of the Land Rover, Ogle shouted. "You can't arrest us; I'm an ex- B Special, Trevor`s an ex- A Special, Percy and Cecil are ex- C Specials and Bobby and Nigel are ex-D Specials." To which the officer responded sneeringly. "Ogle, you`re nicked and now you and your pals are all ex- Porno Specials, so shut the fuck up and get into the wagon." Mickey stood laughing as Ogle and his fellow ex- P Specials were driven down the street and he saw old grumpy Ogle glaring scathingly at him wagging his stubby finger, an expression of pure hatred on his chubby little red face. *What goes around comes around; nosey old codger* he muttered to himself as he quietly closed the door behind him. The following day, as he did each Saturday, went over to Magill's for a few pints. "Christ, Mickey," the barman said, "that was some carry-on in your street last night, apparently Ogle and his cronies were having an orgy, drugs, prostitutes, every slag in the town was there and he got nicked by the peelers." Christy the labourer, who stood at the bar, joined the conversation. "Yeh, Mickey, I heard Ogle and his mates were up before the magistrate this morning and fined fifty pounds each, serves the dirty fuckers right, fuckin` dirt birds that's what they are. A shower of fuckin` dirt birds, I never liked that B Special, Ogle, snidey little bastard, or the rest of his cronies." "Isn't it amazing, Mickey," the barman said, "what goes on behind closed doors and right on your doorstep?" "It certainly is, Billy, it certainly is," he replied smiling, a twinkle in his eye.

Mickey endeavoured to get the requisite monies for the house without success and decided to throw in the towel. He`d sell the house, rent a flat, and that way he`d get Majella back and avoid telling her about the savings, at least for a while. He would go to her mother's house the following Saturday and let her know his decision. On Friday he left work an hour early and went to the Palace Bar, he fancied a few pints by himself to consider how he would handle the situation with Majella the following day. At half-past five, Donal and Peter came charging into the pub. "Mickey, Mickey," Peter shouted wildly, "you're never going to believe this, the union won the case and we`re getting two years back money, almost a year`s wages isn't that incredible." Mickey listening with his mouth agape sprung to his feet knocking over his drink and throwing his arms around Peter screamed. "Jesus, do you know what this means, fucking hell the drinks are on me boys, the drinks are on me." Many, many, drinks later, after his usual trip to the Chinese and off-license, he took a taxi to the new estate to give his wife the good news, even purchasing an extra meal and a bottle of Cork Dry for his mother- in- law. "Mickey," she said, her eyes lighting up on seeing the gin and Chicken Maryland, "you know what you're the best son-in-law in the world so you are and I always knew you were right for Majella, come here now son and give your mother-in-law a big hug." A month later work commenced on their two-up, two-down, and during the couple`s twelve-week stay in her mother's house, Majella became pregnant. Mickey resigned from his job as a bouncer; also giving up smoking on the agreement his wife would stop nagging. Majella chose the

Turquoise Blue bathroom suite over the Jade Green on the basis that the Turquoise Blue better matched the colour of the deep pile shag carpet she`d chosen and after they moved back into their modernised house their first child, a son they called Joseph was born. Paddy Carlin graduated and persuaded Donal to quit his job, the pair opening a flower shop. He reckoned his academic knowledge combined with Donal`s green fingers was a winning combination and he was right; their business thrived and Donal said. "The young people of the town love exotic plants and that's a well-known fact, yes it is." Mickey, after his close encounter with the police that fateful Friday night, never smoked cannabis again although the supply of competitively priced high-quality grass became widely available.

Sammy Ogle sold his house to a young longhaired musician from the city, having received a bullet in the post Ogle decided to move. Billy the barman informed Mickey that one of the neighbours saw Christy the labourer stagger up the cul-de-sac and shove an envelope through Ogle`s letterbox, he was too mean to buy a stamp. So strictly speaking, Ogle did not receive a bullet in the post but rather a bullet through the letterbox. According to the locals, however, this was not a political act; it was because Christy held a bitter grudge against Ogle. He was outraged, believing he was a victim of discrimination, that having spent every Friday night for many years in Magill's bar drinking with Ogle and his chums he was never invited back to Ogle`s house for the ex-special constable`s porno parties.

BORDERLANDS (The Beginning)

The Town, the Mid 1970s

The move from the city to the town was easy, I just said goodbye to my family and friends and left with the firm belief I would be successful and make something of myself. So, while most people deserted the town for the bright lights I had to be different, leaving behind everyone I ever loved and everything I ever knew, making the long journey to the borderlands never to return. Now, the town was a strange place, inhabited by people who were introverted and clannish, the townsfolk like actors on a giant stage, strangers like me bit actors with a walk-on walk-off part, never to play a major role. They were not unfriendly or hostile, just caught up in the place they were born, and would most probably die. My new life was difficult at first as I missed the corner of my hometown, but what I missed most was my friends. When you`re young your friends are everything, defining who you are and helping you make sense of the world. I settled easily into my new job, my colleagues co-operative and helpful, however, I found it strange that of the multitude of people working in the new organisation everyone was from the town except myself and one other important person, but that`s another story and I'll come back to it later.

Anyway, he must have spotted me as I carried my guitars and amplifier into the house. As I locked the car door, I saw him in the mirror sauntering up the street, cigarette dangling from mouth: slouchy, tall, skinny, and dressed in a full-length black leather coat with cowboy hat and pointed boots, silver lone star buckle on belt. "Son," he held out his hand, "you're not from town are you now," he questioned with an impressive American drawl. "No," I replied, "I`m from the city." "And tell me this now, son, what brings a fella like you to the town." "I got a job with the new organisation." "Son, I saw you with a bass guitar, so I've got a proposition for you." "And what`s that now," I queried. "Would you like to join my band, we`re well known around the town and the borderlands playing gigs five or six nights a week?" Now the cowboy got my attention. "And, what do you call your band?" I asked. *The Abraham Lincoln Duo*," he replied, "*The Abe Lincoln Duo* for short, I play the guitar and sing and Skins O Doherty plays the drums, well what do you think now, son?" "I suppose you`d like to hear me play first, you know, to make sure I'm good enough for your band." He shook his head smiling. "No, that won't be necessary at all, you're from the city and city boys are always good players and that's a well-known fact, so it is." "Thank you," I stammered, face blushing as a warm glow rose in my belly. I was in the town only a short time; I had a good job, a house, and now a musician in a successful band, things I could never have achieved in the city, certainly not in such a short period. I noticed him looking at the wheels. "We can use my car if you like." I volunteered eagerly anxious to please the cowboy. "Yes, son, that would be useful, very useful indeed," he replied as I shook his hand. "By the way," he said, "they call me Abe Lincoln

67

but my real name`s Dixie McDermott, and what do they call you now, son?" I told him my name and inquired. "Abe, are you going to change the name of the band?" "Yes, of course, with you onboard from now on we`re *The Abe Lincoln Trio*." So, having met the town cowboy Abe Lincoln, I began my short career as bass guitarist in the popular country and western band *The Abe Lincoln Trio* formerly known as *The Abe Lincoln Duo* travelling the highroads and bye roads of the borderlands playing in small hick country bars with the odd function in larger venues. Knocking out second-rate versions of country and western standards as the punters shimmied and shammied to favourites such as Johnny Cash`s *Ring of Fire* and Patsy Clines *I Fall to Pieces* and smooching the night away to Glen Campbell's *Wichita Linesman* and the like.

Now, a short time before I met Abe I came into ownership of a small terraced house and how this occurred was odd. I was staying in lodgings when the landlady Mrs. Bonner summoned me. "City boy, a close friend of mine, a very special friend indeed," she said blushing as a blood-red tide rose from her ample waxy bosom to her podgy face. "Sammy Ogle is his name and he owns a small, two-up, two- down not far from here and has to move out unexpectedly. We decided the house would suit you fine, so he is letting you have it cheap. He's arranged everything and all you have to do is sign up, you don't even need a deposit. It'll cost you thirty pounds a month the same as your rent here." I jumped at the chance of having my own place; however, when I went to sign what I assumed was a lease it turned out I was purchasing the property outright much to my pleasant surprise. The owner receiving a bullet in the post had to vacate in a hurry and arranged all the paperwork and mortgage, which suited me fine, I learned with the right contacts anything was possible in the town. Sammy Ogle essentially hoodwinked me into buying my first home, and signing the dotted line I moved in the next day, the day I met Abe. The residents of the street were elderly except for Mickey and Majella Coyle who lived with their son Joe a few doors down who were friendly; the rest of the neighbours simply ignored me being wary of strangers. What I loved most about my house was its proximity to the local corner bar called Magill's. This dilapidated establishment comprised a small public house with, shabby interior, varnished timber sheeted walls adorned with a variety of bevelled mirrors advertising a range of local whiskies. Red leather perimeter seating peppered with cigarette burns, dirty stained carpet, and the sweet sticky smell of spilled beer with the lingering odour of stale cigarette smoke and the faint tang of urine clinging in the air. I remember my first visit well. I approached the bar where the owner Billy Cleary, a small portly man wearing an oversized starched white apron, stood behind the counter washing glasses. "What are yeh having, son", he asked in a relaxed welcoming manner. "A pint of Guinness, please," I replied. And, as he meticulously, without making eye contact, poured the drink commenced a litany of questions. "You're not from the town now are you, son." It began and by the time he finished, placing a beautifully sculptured pint of majestic perfection before me, he knew my life story. I became a regular at Magill's and every evening, tired and hungry after work, I would call in for a bottle or two of Red Hand stout and a processed beef burger, cooked in the new cutting edge microwave oven, which was cardboard tasting, soggy, and barely edible. However, the addition of copious amounts of tomato sauce giving the burger some flavour, but only just. The regulars were friendly enough, and I soon discovered endowed with a bizarre sense of humour. I recall at Christmas when Chris Mc Kenna, a history teacher from the college, came charging into the bar waving a large white envelope. "Fire in the hole, fire in the hole," he shouted excitedly to which one of the punters, Packy Mc Daid, acerbic wit honed by eight pints of Guinness and a couple of Paddy whiskey chasers, returned sharply. "What professor, were yeh on the Vindaloo last night," the bar exploding into rapturous laughter. "Ah, shut the fuck up, Mc Daid, yeh thick slabbering clampit," Chris retorted. "I got one, I got one," he hollered ecstatically, "I got a bullet in the post, and it came in a beautiful Christmas card." He proudly passed the bullet and card around the drinkers who ran their fingers lovingly over the full metal jacket and I gazed in utter astonishment as an elderly woman held the bullet to her lips adoringly and gently kissed it. Nearly falling off my barstool in disbelief when I saw the Christmas card that read: *Peace, Love, and Goodwill to all Christian men.* Chris Mc Kenna was honoured to have received the card meaning that someone had gone to a lot of trouble and expense. When I asked him if he felt threatened, he laughed it off. "No, city boy, not at all why should I, sure if they were going to shoot me why would they bother sending the bullet in the post." However, despite the many enjoyable and humorous nights spent in Magill`s I had one bad experience when a young guy called Charlie Devine cornered me in the toilets on a Saturday night and poking me hard in the chest spouted. "Hey you, city boy, tell me now what the fuck are you doing in our town, are you a spy or something coming here and taking our jobs, you're walking on thin fucking ice, mucker, why don't you just fuck off back to the city where you belong, you're not welcome here."

One Saturday afternoon, as I was painting the living room, Abe or to be more correct Dixie Mc Dermott called around. "What about yeh, son," he said, "we`ve hit the jackpot, we`re the bee`s knees and by the way, I like the colour of that paint, what`s it called now?" "Autumn Brown, Abe," I replied. "Nice colour and a nice ring to the name, I might just get the missus to redecorate our house it could do with a lick of paint, so it could. Anyway, as I was saying we've hit the jackpot big time; we're going up in the world. At last my talents as an entertainer in the town have been recognised; we`ve got the regular Friday and Saturday nightspot in *The Sputnik Bar* in the new estate. The monies great, free drink, and we can leave our gear in the bar over the weekend."Accordingly, every Friday and Saturday night we performed in *The Sputnik Bar* playing upstairs in what was called *The Singing Lounge* that was packed at the weekend as the bar was the only venue in the new estate providing entertainment. *The Sputnik Bar,* however, was an establishment with a reputation, a very bad reputation indeed. This was the height of the troubles and the reason we were paid so well was that no other band would venture into the new estate that was a republican-controlled area. As the weeks passed and we settled in I noticed a young man who sat close to the stage during the gigs eyeing me intently and over time wangled his way into my company. He told me his name was Chinky Mc Laughlin and asked me to teach him to play the bass, which I did. For a while, I pestered Abe to let me perform a couple of rock and roll songs during the break and finally, he agreed. Chinky accompanied me while I sang and played lead guitar, the crowd loving our rendition of *Johnny Be Good* and *Summer Time Blues,* even Skins the drummer enjoyed playing rock and roll. Chinky's friends began to frequent the bar and, as he became more proficient on the bass, we added a couple of new songs to our repertoire each week as a well-oiled Abe sat at the bar drinking copious double Powers Gold Label whiskeys and banging his glass on the counter shouting, *"more, more, more."* I came to enjoy the gigs, free drink, a chance to play rock and roll, and the odd lucky occasion when I scored with one of Chinky`s female friends who would accompany me back to the house. One Saturday night, I threw a housewarming party and invited Chinky and his friends (excluding Abe and Skins) back after the gig. I even invited Mickey and Majella, on the basis that if the neighbours complained Mickey would sort it out, but the couple didn't come stating they couldn't get a babysitter. Armed with numerous brown paper bags of carryout's, Buckfast tonic wine, multiple cans of beer, and Chinky clutching a bottle of Drambuie liqueur, his favourite tipple, a group of rambunctious youngsters congregated in my house and to the sounds of Janis Joplin, Grace Slick, Grannies Intentions and Frank Zappa pumping from my record player got drunk. Dancing away all our troubles in the small house that was to be my home, at least for a short time. As I engaged in deep meaningful conversation with Paddy Carlin the local florist, a young girl tapped me on the shoulder. "Hey, city boy, you'd better go after him, he`s off on one of his wild rampages." "Who is," I asked annoyance in my voice, "that glory boy, Chinky," she replied, "you know what he's like when he's on the Drambuie." "No, I don't," I responded dryly, "but I`m sure I`m about to find out, where did he go?" "He lifted your sledgehammer, took off his shirt, tied it around his head, and charged down the street talking to himself in some funny language, you better go and find him God knows what he'll do, I've seen him in action before." The sledgehammer in question I borrowed from Mickey when he invited me to see his house of which he was extremely proud, and I must confess the bathroom was amazing. Turquoise Blue coloured plastic bathroom suite and shower, blue shag pile carpet, blue fluffy toilet seat cover, blue plastic curtains, all matching accessories, and as I stood spellbound, awash in a sea of greenish-blue, I decided I was building an extension and Mickey lent me a sledgehammer to commence knocking down a few walls, my youthful enthusiasm knowing no bounds. "Jesus, city boy," she continued, "you'd better get moving, Chinky`s wired to the moon he`s a proper fuckin` moon dog, the drink sends him doolally." I bolted down the street

73

towards the town centre but nothing-not a soul. After half an hour, I turned back when I saw, with the corner of my eye, a figure telephone in hand standing at a first-floor window of the house next to where Donal Devine lived. It was the silhouette of an old doll looking towards Magill's on the corner facing her house. Glancing over I noticed the side street adjacent to the pub littered with shards of glass reflected in the moonlight and rushing over peered through the window, the interior illuminated by the orange glow of street lights, and saw him lying on the bar counter, a serene grin on face, sledgehammer in hand, covered in blood. I jumped into the bar. "Right, Kemosabe, come on now back to the reservation for you, yeh fuckin` idiot." And, getting him out onto the pavement I dragged him to the house. "Everyone," I shouted, "the party`s over, grab your gear and fuck off home." I lay Chinky on the couch and spent the night watching him toss and turn, grunting, growling, and mumbling incoherently, as I awaited a loud knock on the door, but nothing. However, what worried me was Billy Cleary, he knew where I lived, and I had mentioned in passing I was having a party. I waited patiently until midday and decided to go to the bar and bluff it out, any accusations I would deny, saying I went to bed early drunk and saw nothing, and by this time I was ravenous for a greasy burger slathered in red sauce accompanied by a few Red Hands to wash it down. So, strolling nonchalantly over to Magill`s I brazenly entered. The first thing I noticed was the boarded-up window and the splattered blood stains. As I approached the bar, fear mingled with apprehension, Billy, who was washing blood from the counter, glanced up without speaking. "What's happened, Billy," I asked nervously?" "Ah, that fucker Charlie Devine broke into the bar last night, but not to worry the woman across the street called the police and they nabbed him climbing out the window with a load of cigarettes and drink. He'll do time for this the robbin` little bastard just look at the mess he left, anyway, son, what are yeh having?" "Same as usual, Billy," I replied, relief in my voice. "A bottle of Red Hand and a burger, actually, Billy, make it two burgers, I`m feckin`starving." The following week, Donal Devine called at my house. "Listen, city boy," he said, "I`m sure you heard my brother Charlie was done by the cops for breaking into Magill's. He was passing and the window was smashed so he climbed in helping himself to goodies, however, didn't the police arrive and catch him red-handed, but here's the funny thing, someone had already broken into the bar and got away scot-free, isn't that incredible, Christ talk about bad luck. Now, city boy, my partner Paddy Carlin was at your party and saw that idiot hell-raising fucker Chinky Mc Laughlin covered in blood holding a sledgehammer. Tell me now, this is important and could stop my brother from getting a jail sentence, was it Mc Laughlin who broke into the bar, I want the truth, city boy?" "No," I returned assertively, "no way, Chinky was pissed out of his mind, absolutely hammered, too drunk to stand up straight. I found him down the back alley, he'd cut himself when he fell." I'm not sure if he believed me or not but a few weeks later I met Mickey in the bar who informed me that Charlie Devine was sentenced to six months in prison and for some reason he was delighted. "Serves that fucker right," he said smiling, "he'd that coming for a long time, so he has. Here have a pint it's on me I'm celebrating, although the one thing I don't understand is this. Charlie Devine hadn't a scratch on him yet the bar was covered in blood, strange that isn't it?" He looked squarely at me a cheeky grin on his face. "And tell me this, city boy, what do you think of Devine doing time?" "Well, Mickey," I replied tongue in cheek, "I genuinely believe that what goes around comes around, and that mouth almighty Devine got what he deserved if you see what I mean." "Your right there, city boy, dead on, I'll drink to that, so I will."

Chinky never mentioned the sledgehammer incident nor did I, and over time our friendship grew closer. I saw something of myself in him; I was a stranger in the town but in many ways, so was he. He took me into his confidence revealing things about the place others wouldn't. He was unemployed, his father and brother were unemployed, half the men in the town were unemployed and because of their religion and politics treated by the ruling elite as second-class citizens and the people were angry, and nobody embodied this anger more than the irascible, Chinky. He loved to drink and drink heavily, usually from a half-pint glass full to the brim of sweet yellow Drambuie which he`d purchase on receipt of his weekly dole money or occasionally when funds were low Buckfast tonic wine, and when wreaking havoc with great exuberance he'd shout. "The Bucky made me do it, the Bucky made me do it," and when drunk he`d do outrageous things to express his anger. Accepted by

Chinky and his friends, to a certain degree, my past life a fading memory as I experienced how wonderful it was to wear the golden crown of acceptance. I was on a roll, job, house, part-time musician, and new friends. I was running the table, however, this changed dramatically one Saturday night. It was a holiday weekend, Easter as far as I recall, and Chinky and his friends had gone on a free coach trip to some republican celebration in the borderlands, more like a drinking session I'm sure. However, it was business as usual in *The Sputnik Bar, The Singing Lounge* packed to overflowing, everyone in a holiday mood the air crackling with excitement. About an hour into our set all hell broke loose, *The Singing Lounge* erupting as the crowd with a tumultuous roar leapt to their feet, the room reverberating to the sound of stomping and banging of glasses. From the stage, I saw a well-dressed woman and a bearded man make their way towards the bar surrounded by an ecstatic cheering mob. "Who is it, Abe?" I shouted, barely audible above the din. "I don't know, but I'll soon find out," and jumping off the stage he pushed his way through the heaving mass and minutes later a flushed Abe returned. "It's Doctor Rose Dugdale and all the top-notch republican boys, it`s magic, son, pure fuckin` magic," he shouted. "Who`s Rose Dugdale?" I asked naively. "She`s a hero, a hero to the people of the town." "Why, Abe?" "I stuttered, and shaking his head with incredulity replied, "Jesus Christ, son, you worry me at times because she dropped fuckin` bombs on the peelers in Strabane Police Station from a helicopter, can you believe it, bombed the black bastards right in their rat's nest, hit the fuckers hard. What a

77

spectacular, she's on the run and I just can't believe it, she's right here in *The Sputnik* and we're playing, Jesus Christ, son, this is the best night of my life." I never saw Abe as animated before as he charged around the stage punching the air, even Skins was jumping up and down like a jack in the box banging on his snare drum as I stood impassive failing to grasp the magnitude of the occasion. Abe grabbed the microphone. "Come on, guys; let's belt out a few rebel songs." "I don't know any, Abe," I gushed apologetically. Nevertheless, without replying Abe dropped his cowboy persona and began a lively medley of rousing republican songs, but no sooner had he started when someone dived onto the stage grabbed the microphone screaming. "It`s a raid, it`s a raid, the peelers are here, the peelers are here," as Rose Dugdale and her entourage bolted for the door shouting. "Run to fuck, run to fuck, run for your lives," the fleeing desperados disappearing in seconds down the stairs. Minutes later uproar as a lone soldier clad in full riot gear and clutching a CS gas gun stood at the lounge door, the sight of which caused hullaballoo, driving the hoard into a frenzied rabble baying for blood as a cascade of bottles, chairs, and tables hurled at the terrified squaddie who scampered down the stairs like a frightened rabbit running for his life. An eerie silence descended over the lounge shattered by thunderous cracks as several CS gas canisters came flying into the room filling the air with a thick poisonous gas and all pandemonium broke loose, the punters gasping for breath, skin burning scurried wildly around the lounge. In frenzied desperation, they charged en- masse toward the exit to find the staircase blocked with broken furniture, the floor littered with glass. I kicked open the fire escape door inhaling deeply on the cold night air as Abe and Skins dived past me followed by a scrambling melee of people who teeming forward, screaming and shouting, piled onto the metal staircase disappearing into the darkness. Finally, when the lounge bar emptied, I grabbed my guitar and struggling for breath clambered down the escape to be confronted by a solitary black soldier in riot gear, deathly-looking baton in hand. Later, I found out that everyone escaping down the stairs struck hard including elderly men and women with some hospitalised. I saw the menace in his eyes as he lifted the baton to strike. "Musician," I mumbled, raising my guitar. He stared at me blankly unable to understand my city accent accentuated by trembling voice. He hesitated and I uttered, "Bob Marley." I saw a flicker in his eye. "Yeah, man, I`m from Brixton, love the reggae vibe, now fuck off, Paddy," so Paddy fucked off. As I limped home, feet cut by broken glass; I heard the distant *rattle, rattle* of a Thompson machine gun in the night air. I knew the republicans would strike back after all it was their turf. *That's that idiot, Scatter O Doherty, with that old rusty Thompson of his, firing at everything and never hitting anything and no wonder; he'd spent the night drinking heavily in The Sputnik and steaming drunk barely able to stand.*

The next day I drove to Abe`s house to tell him we should cancel the gig at *The Sputnik* after last night's disturbance. His wife opened the door, paintbrush in hand, face, and clothes splattered with paint. Abe was in the kitchen, which stunk of cigarette smoke, red lacquered Hohner guitar in one hand, beer in the other, cigarette hanging from his mouth. "Abe," I said, "I need to talk to you, I think it`s too dangerous for us to play in *The Sputnik*." He sat back staring fixedly at me. "Son, I'm glad you're here, I've been meaning to talk to you, so I have. Skins and me had a band meeting this morning and we decided you're sacked, we don't need you anymore." I stood crestfallen; his words piercing me like a sharp knife. "But, why, Abe," I sputtered as a wave of disappointment and hurt swept through my body. "Well, son, it's like this you don't fit in now, do you. You let me down last night and to tell the truth, you're not really one of us are you now, son. You were only ever in the band because of your wheels, but we don't need them anymore from now on we`re playing in *The Sputnik* five nights a week, isn't that just brilliant and by the way, what do you think of the wife's paint job, I sure do love that Autumn Brown?" As I turned to leave without replying, he called after me. "Son, I forgot to mention, that pal of yours, Chinky, he`s taking your place in the band."

The following week I opened the door to two scrawny teenagers. "City boy, I`m Feargal and this is my cousin Kevin. A friend of ours, Chinky Mc Laughlin, told us you have guitars and an amplifier you don`t need so we want to buy them, we've formed a band." I stepped back in surprise. "Did he now," I snapped, "well, I suppose I don't need them anymore, you can have them if the monies right." As they struggled down the hill hauling the guitars and amplifier, I called after them. "Feargal, tell me what`s the name of your new band?" "We haven't got a name yet, but we`re a punk rock band and were going to be famous, by the way we`re playing our first gig in Ken Gunne`s bar *The Casbah* next week, why don't you come along your old friend Chinky will be there." "Thanks anyway, Feargal, but I think I'll give that one a miss if you don't mind and good luck with your new band," I responded wryly as I closed the door. *Punk Rock, Christ, what will they think of next?*

BORDERLANDS (The End)

With my part-time job as a musician ended I focused on my career determined to progress in the organisation. A senior position became available which suited me and well within my capabilities. I applied for the role and set about preparing meticulously for the interview gleaning all the information I deemed useful and it was my expectation I would be successful. The day of reckoning came and I nervously entered the room where five of them sat staring impassively at me, five dour faces with five dour expressions. "Sit there," the top woman commanded gruffly, gesturing to a chair on the opposite side of the table from the dour faces. I sat, hands on knees, eyes fixed squarely on the top woman. She spoke at me as the others sat silent, doodling, stringently avoiding eye contact. She rambled on about the difficulties associated with the job, questioning my capabilities and when I briefly lost concentration, she hit me with an awkward question. Randomly, one of the dour faces threw me a meaningless query. "What book are you reading at the moment," and, "where do you think you`ll be in twenty years?" to which I gave a half-hearted indignant response. I knew this was not a proper interview and the top woman was trying to humiliate me, but for what reason? "Any questions," she barked when finished her monotonous monologue. "No,"

I replied curtly and turning headed briskly towards the door without acknowledging the five dour faces with the five dour expressions. I drove home and went straight to the pub. Billy was surprised. "Hello, son, never seen you on the grog at this time before, hope you're not developing bad habits now?" "Billy, I need a drink, give me a whiskey with a drop of water and make it a double, pick a good one for me." I chugged back the whiskey in one greedy glug. "Are you okay, son?" Billy inquired." "Ah, nothing," I replied despondently, "I had my mind set on a job, I believed it was perfect for me. I was sure I`d get the position but the interview went badly, to be honest, it wasn't a real interview at all. But that`s the way things go, you win some and lose some, same again, Billy." He handed me the drink. "Here, son, it's on the house." "Thank you, thank you very much." Billy leaned on the bar arms folded and looked me straight in the eye. "Son, a word to the wise. Now you're a clever ambitious young man and you'll go far in the world, but not in the town." I reeled back in disbelief devastated by his words. "What do you mean, Billy, what the hell are you talking about?" "Listen, son, things are difficult here what with unemployment and the political situation, harder than most places, opportunities are few and far between and strangers don't fare too well and that`s the God`s truth." I could not believe what I was hearing, I`d got it all wrong, how could I have been so stupid. He caught the look of bewilderment on my face. "Son, I came to the town in the long-ago from the borderlands as an apprentice barman. I was like you a total stranger with ambition and drive, worked in every pub in the town, got to know the people well, understood their hopes and dreams. Then the phone call came, an uncle of mine died in America and left me a fortune; unexpectedly my dream came true. I could buy a bar and be my own boss, all the things I ever wanted in this world. Now, son that sounds easy doesn't it, nevertheless, could I buy a bar in the town, no way! Every time a bar was for sale, I put in a generous offer, but every time I missed the boat and a higher offer made, all sort of bullshit. The reality was simple, the bar owners in the town didn't want me, a stranger like you, to own a pub and do well and me working here twenty years. In the end, I bought a pub through the back door; so to speak, sure didn't I pay someone to buy this bar for me." "Jesus, Billy, are you for real, are you telling me I'm wasting my time in the town, here give us another drink for God's sake, I can't believe all this crap." The large intake of strong liquor in the daytime made me light-headed and I found it difficult to concentrate. What was he saying and what did he mean? "Billy, let me get this straight, you're saying the people of the town keep everything for themselves, the businesses, the jobs?" "Yes, son," he replied, "that's generally what the people with money and power try to do when they can, they try to keep strangers out and that`s the gist of it alright. I'm surprised you landed a post in the organisation at all, now that was a fluke." "But, how can they do that, Billy, it's impossible." "Is it," he returned sharply. "Of course it is," I replied. "Listen, son, why in God`s name would I lie to you?" "I don't know, Billy, but it's not true?" "Not true," he responded sarcastically. "But, what do you mean, Billy?" He gestured towards the back of the bar where three men sat in the far corner sipping pints of stout, glaring ominously back at me. One of the men called out. "Hey, city boy, come down here now and join us and by the way, it's your round." They caught me lovely, so I bought a round of drinks and joined them. I knew the men; they worked in the organisation as labourers and the one I knew best, Christy O Doherty, spoke. "Tell me now, why the fancy duds, city boy?" He questioned, slurring his words. "I had a job interview, Christy," I replied. "Did you now, city boy, the same interview as Dopey Donavan." The men burst into spontaneous laughter. "Now, city boy, let's get this right. You'd an interview for the job Dopey Donavan got, he works with us in the depot, he`s a lorry driver." "No, Christy," I replied defensively a wistful smile on my face, "you must be mistaken this was for a senior managerial post in head office." They collectively burst into hysterics and by this time, I was feeling uneasy. "As I`ve said, city boy, Dopey got the job, but I haven't told you the funny bit yet." "But, Christy," I spluttered agitation in my voice, "the interviews were this afternoon, how would he know he got the job?" More hysterics and banging of fists, a full pint of stout spilling over the table. "Sorry, city boy, we can see you're upset, but, to tell the truth, so are we. That fucker Donavan is a thick as two short planks, so he is, couldn't manage a drinking session in a fuckin` brewery, sure the fucker can hardly write his name and now he`s got the manager's job he`ll think he`s better than the rest of us." Suitably mortified I stood in a cold rage and walked briskly towards the exit. "Good night, Billy," I said weakly avoiding eye contact, and as I opened the door Christy shouted after me. "Hey, city boy, hold on a minute you haven't heard the best bit yet." I stopped and wheeled around agog at what he would say. "Dopey Donavan, he knew he got the job a month ago, the top woman told him so." A world of tears rose in my eyes as I thundered down to the river, sitting awhile on a wooden bollard and under pale moonlight watched my hopes and dreams bobbing angrily on the dark choppy waters, cursing the town and its people. Billy was right; there was no place for me here, no place for strangers, so I decided to leave. As I walked home the heavens opened, the raindrops bouncing off the pavement echoing the storm raging in my soul.

It was my last Friday working for the organisation with one final task to complete. A businessman from the borderlands had to abandon his home and move to the town, and I arranged his accommodation the previous week at which time he told me he`d been threatened. "Did you get a bullet in the post," I enquired naively. He threw me a look of puzzlement. "No, I didn't," he replied sharply, so I changed the subject. My last duty was to call at the property to ensure the businessman was satisfied with his accommodation. "Hope you like your new house," I said enthusiastically as I walked around the property and randomly opening a bedroom cupboard door, I stepped back mouth agape horrified at what it contained. Confronting me was an M 1 assault rifle, the type favoured by republicans in the town. I stood mesmerised by the shiny black killing machine-standing sentinel before me until he broke the silence. "Nothing to report here, son," he said threateningly, slamming the door shut. "No, the files closed on this property, sir," I replied with foolish words. I did not return to work as I intended to bid farewell to my colleagues but instead went to Magill's bar. "Are you okay, son?" Billy inquired, "you're as white as a sheet." "Billy, give me a double whiskey you know the one I like, and have one yourself." I sat in the seat normally occupied by the labourers pondering my predicament. I`d a problem, a big problem indeed! My time in the town taught me many things, so I was fully aware of my serious quandary and as the whiskey charged my brain, I considered my options. If I did nothing the rifle would be used to shoot a policeman or soldier or even one of the ruling elite and I didn't want blood on my hands. I could inform the police who would seize the weapon and arrest the businessman who would come after me, the fact I was leaving meant nothing. They would hunt me down as an informer, torture and kill me and I did not want to spend the rest of my life looking over my shoulder. Feeling comfortably numb with the support of a couple more doubles of smooth ten-year-old pot still Green Spot, it came to me: the solution to my dilemma.

Monday morning I drove to the organization's head office and knocked on the top woman's door, entered her office where she sat reading the morning's newspaper nursing a mug of steaming coffee. "Top woman, you know I've resigned my post and leaving the town," I said with a faint whiff of indignation. "Yes," she replied, "I`m sorry but it can't be helped, can it now?" I stood puzzled by her enigmatic words. "Top woman," I continued, "there`s something important I have to tell you before I go." "And what`s that now, son," she inquired, looking at me over her gold-framed glasses. "I`ve got a dilemma, top woman." She studied me with interest. "Really, and what dilemma is that now, son?" "The dilemma I`m going to hand over to you right now, top woman," I replied boldly as I passed her the green file explaining that while inspecting a property I discovered an assault rifle in a cupboard and having left the organisation I was handing the case over to her to decide what action to take regarding the shiny black killing machine. "Also, top woman, I told the businessman I was leaving and handing the case over to you, I also gave him your contact details so he knows where to find you if any issues arise." As I turned to leave, she summoned me back. "Son, I'll handle this case it`s no longer your concern, it`s my responsibility now. But, there's something I want to say before you go." "And, what's that, top woman?" I inquired. "About the interview a few weeks ago, the job you applied for, it wasn't meant for you." "But, why?" I asked as she glanced down at the headlines on the morning paper. "You were by far the best qualified and most suitable candidate for the job, but the truth is I didn't want you to have it." Her words pierced my soul like a dagger. "But, why, I don't understand, top woman?" She glanced up from the newspaper. "Son, I knew you'd leave the town if you didn't get the job your pride would make you. The person I gave it to needed it more than you, where could he go?" I`d heard enough and as I turned to depart she called after me. "It`s for your own good, son, like you I came here from the city, so I had to help you leave before it was too late, goodbye and good luck to you now."

Everything became clear; she didn't want me to get the job because just like her, I would be trapped in the town never fulfilling my destiny, a stranger amongst the people, never fully accepted, and no matter how long you lived there, never truly at home.

THE LAST BUS

Belfast, the 1970s

Sergeant John Murray glanced at the office clock that read half-past eight, he'd been on duty for twelve hours and was tired and hungry. For the past year, he`d worked long shifts, six days a week, always first in, always last home. Closing the file on his latest case, he put on his coat, turned off the lights in the office he shared with five other anti-terrorist police officers and locked the door behind him. As he drove through the security gates of the heavily fortified police station, he stopped the car and wound down the window. "Bad night, Tom, I feel sorry for you out in weather like this." The police officer on guard duty bent down and peered through the window, droplets of rainwater cascading down the shiny peak of his cap onto his face. "Sure is, sergeant, not a night for standing here but someone's got to do it, you never know when the bastards will strike next, they're hitting us everywhere these days and they're armed to the teeth." "Good night, Tom," he replied softly as he eased the heavy Triumph Acclaim onto the deserted main road. *What will it be tonight, a fish supper or a Chinese takeaway?* Settling for a fish supper, as the chip shop was next door to the off-license; he stuffed the newspaper-wrapped fish and chips under his overcoat and entered the off-license. "Good evening, sergeant", the grey-haired shop assistant greeted him cheerfully, "see you're working late again." "No rest for the wicked, Willie," he replied, slipping a bottle of Black Bush into his pocket. "You must be busy with all the killings, sergeant." "Rough times, Willie, rough times indeed, I just don't know where it`s all going to end and that`s the truth of it." "Well, sergeant, at least our side is giving the Taigs a taste of their own medicine and it's about time too if you know what I mean." *I know exactly what you mean* he muttered to himself as he left the shop without replying. Driving home, he tuned into the police frequency. *Christ, another body found, another innocent young man hacked to pieces, murdering bastards that`s what they all were, murdering bastards the lot of them.* He parked outside his house-the house that was once his home. A small two-story property in the east of the city where they lived all their married life and having no children a garden or extra space was never needed, so the house suited the couple fine. He opened the front door, stepped into the hall that was cold and musty with the faint smell of damp and decay, and closing the door behind him stood in the dark expecting her to call from the bedroom above. "Home, at last, my big, strong, handsome policeman, come up here now and show your wife how much you love her." He would arrive home in the early hours of the morning chilled to the bone and she`d be waiting for him, the bed warm and her soft body tender and inviting. "And make sure you take off those size tens," she`d shout as he rushed up the stairs to hold her and love her and let the exertions of a long night`s shift tramping the cold deserted streets vanish, melting into a sea of softness, loveliness, and warmth. He shivered; the living room was a mess, empty whiskey bottle and the remnants of the previous night's half-eaten Chinese meal on the coffee table. Knelling, he turned on the two-bar electric heater and reaching over switched on the small television set which sat in the corner beside the fireplace. Without taking off his coat he sat heavily on the couch, pulled off his boots, placing his service revolver on the table and, on opening the newspaper, devoured the lukewarm, greasy battered fish and soggy chips without cutlery, washed down with a large measure of Black Bush, which he drank from a dirty tumbler. When finished he poured another large measure of whiskey and slumped back trying to focus on the flickering black and white images dancing across the television screen. The food and drink made him groggy and falling into a deep slumber snoring gently only to be rudely awoken at around half past six by the clanking of milk bottles, the television flickering and the electric fire glowing red. Rubbing sleepiness from his eyes, he slid uneasily off the couch back aching. *Christ, I`ll have to start sleeping in my own bed again, this couch is far too* *small for me.* He stretched himself before clambering up the narrow timber stairs for a cold shower, a shave, and a change of shirt and underwear. He hated going into what was once their bedroom, he could smell her perfume and sense her presence, and glancing at their marital bed the memories came flooding back. While, as a hardnosed policeman he was sceptical about the afterlife and such matters, he could sense her presence in the bedroom finding it unbearable to enter the room, and the reason he chose to sleep in the living room.

On entering the empty office, he made a mug of strong coffee before beginning his day's work. The sergeant and his colleagues were finding it impossible to cope with the number of murders on their patch; simply overwhelmed and unable to investigate properly each killing, working six days a week without holidays, with Sunday the sergeant's day of rest. Sunday would begin with service at the Cherry Valley Presbyterian Church, then he'd leave his laundry with his next-door neighbour, Sadie a widow, to wash, dry, and iron, placing the clean clothes neatly in a bedroom cupboard, enough clothes, and underwear for a week. On the odd occasion she might prepare Sunday lunch for him, but often or not he`d go to a city-centre hotel if any were still open. But, the most important thing he did on his day off was to visit his wife's grave on which he would place a bouquet of beautiful flowers, red roses her favourite. He would kneel at the graveside and speak to his wife. "Eileen, my darling, I want you to know I'm doing fine, I`m eating well, and yes, I do take off the size tens before going up the stairs and, yes, I do have a clean shirt and underwear every day." He would tell her how much he loved her and how much he missed her and it came as a shock when he received a visit from an old friend from Special Branch. "John, an informer in the west of the city advised us an I.R.A. spotter has picked up on your weekly visits to the cemetery and a death squad is waiting to hit you, so the weekly ritual has to stop. Sergeant," he continued, "If you visit your wife`s grave you`ll end up visiting her in heaven and that`s a fact. "But Sam," the sergeant replied despondently. "It`s the most important thing in my life, you know it`s all I live for." "Sergeant, I understand, but if you insist on visiting the grave we`ll have to put a major security operation in place. We'd need helicopters and the army to cordon off the area; it would be a logistical nightmare. Do you know the resources it would take to protect you, and with the bloody loyalist and their murder gangs on the loose, we`re stretched to the limit? We can do nothing now, sergeant, when things calm down a bit I will see what I can do. We could take you in an armoured car or something, in the meantime do not venture near the graveyard it's far too dangerous and that's an order from the top; we can't afford to lose someone of your calibre." The poignancy of his colleague's words kept running through his mind- *If you visit your wife's grave you'll end up visiting her in heaven.*

A pile of papers sat on his desk giving details of the previous night's gruesome murder, always the same, always a similar pattern. A young Catholic man goes out for a drink and is abducted by a loyalist gang on his way home and brutally murdered. A wall of silence surrounding each death, the police unable to do anything except process the paperwork and move on to the next killing. Each murder more vicious than the last. They'd stopped shooting their victims instead resorting to the use of hammers, butcher knives- anything to make the slaughter as brutal and inhumane as possible, their sole objective was to terrorise Catholics. He saw it every day on the loyalist murals *Kill all Taigs and let God sort them out* and *Irish Out*. The republicans were waging a vicious bloody war against the security forces and in the eyes of loyalists; every Catholic was guilty no matter how innocent you were. While he understood loyalists taking the war to republicans, slaughtering innocent people? He glanced at the photographs of the latest victim, eighteen years old, unemployed, almost decapitated, slamming the file shut in disgust. *Loyalists, loyal to what, butchering innocent young men in the name of the Queen, for God and country. How could a small*

Christian place like Ulster produce men capable of such obscene violence? The bigotry and sectarianism of the city shocked him. He was from a farming background in Fermanagh, a quiet rural backwater where both traditions respected each other and didn't blame each other for what happened in the past. Even the bigoted entrenched views of his colleagues stunned him and them all church-going men, pillars of society with strong Christian beliefs and the extreme views of the inspector and him running the station. Where would it all end? It got more violent and uncontrollable daily, and although the police knew who the killers were it was impossible to get witnesses to testify against them. The inspector interrupted his thoughts. "Sergeant, I want you and a constable to go over to the drinking club in the loyalist area, we've heard from a tout some of the murder gang drink there. It's a waste of time but at least it's something to let them know we're on the case, give them something to think about." "Okay, inspector, I'm on my way." When they reached the club, the sergeant turned to the young policeman. "Constable, you wait in the car this shouldn't take too long." "Are you sure, sergeant," he replied, concern in his voice. "Yes, constable, if I'm not out in fifteen minutes come and get me and make sure to call for backup." The loyalist-drinking den was dark, dingy, reeking of stale beer and cigarette smoke. Two longhaired youths clad in denim playing snooker abandoned their game slinking past as he entered. At the bar, a big, bespectacled, corpulent man, dressed in a black leather jacket and jeans sat pint in hand in deep conversation with the barman their discussion ending abruptly on seeing the sergeant. "Well, now, and what have we got here, shouldn't you be out chasing terrorists, sergeant?" the big man said mockingly. "What can we do for you?" the barman asked in a softer tone, "and by the way, sergeant, would you like a wee one while you're here?" The sergeant nodded and turned to the big man. "We know some of the murder gang drink here; you wouldn't happen to know the killers would you now?" The big man slid off his stool and swaggered towards the sergeant. "And what murder gang is that you're referring to?" The sergeant finished his whiskey in one gulp. "You know fine well what I'm talking about, Christ do you not realise the carnage you're causing across the city." "Listen, mister policeman, I'll tell you what we're doing, we're doing your job for you's ones, the ordinary Protestant working folk is going after the terrorists." "Working folk," the sergeant replied angrily, "your crowd never worked a day in their lives, and the young fella you butchered last night, got his head cut off, he was no terrorist just an innocent man in the wrong place at the wrong time." The big man laughed. "Listen, policeman, none of them Taigs are innocent and you should know that now in your line of work, Catholics are all terrorists trying to destroy our wee God-given country and drive us out and what are you lot doing about it, sitting on your hands, pussyfooting around the murderers and the bombers, that's what you're doing. And, sergeant, that's not good enough now, you have to fight fire with fire and that's what the lads are doing, bringing the war to the Johnny Rebs." "Listen, big man, you don't know the mayhem you're causing with the slaughter of innocent people, our resources are stretched to the limit without your lot getting involved, you're making the security situation worse." "We're going to win this war, sergeant," the big man scowled defiantly, "no matter what it takes with or without your help. We are the people and we'll drive the Taigs out of our country, our rightful homeland. And remember, sergeant, you're either with us or against us, there's no in-between, do you hear me now?" He picked up his glass finishing his beer in one greedy swallow. "Sergeant, there's a friend of mine an Englishman, Oxford-educated, who comes in here now and again for a few sherries. Now, he served in the army all over the world and he knows a thing or two about the colonies and he tells me that we lost our empire by the softly, softly approach. But we're not going to lose this part of our United Kingdom to the Paddies, remember Ulster is British and not part of Ireland, that's the priest-ridden state down south, not here, and that stupid made-up leprechaun language of theirs, Fenian scum that's all they are. He says, my friend the Englishman, they're all the same, the Wogs, the Pakis, the

Paddies, no difference, all they understand is force and terror. You have to keep them in their place otherwise; they get ideas above their station. Sure, look what happened in India and the other colonies. Now, my friend knows Brigadier Kitson who`s an expert in these matters and has taught him a few special persuasion techniques for dealing with the Paddies and he tells me he and his colleagues are using these effectively." Sergeant Murray banged his fist on the bar counter. "Listen, big man," he shouted, "I`m going to get every last one of you murdering bastards, I`ll leave no stone unturned until every one of you is behind bars." The big man stepped back staring fixedly at the sergeant. "Are you now," he said in a low ominous voice, "I don't like your attitude policeman, Taig lover; I don't like your attitude at all. We have friends in high places even in the government, here and across the water, no one can stop us; no one's big enough to get in our way." As the sergeant turned towards the door, the big man called after him. "Hold on a minute, Sergeant Murray, I haven't finished yet. We have to defend Britain and the end justifies the means, that`s why we're called Great Britain. What fucking right have the thick Paddies to challenge us, us the chosen people, the cheek of the dirty fuckers?" "Listen, big man," the sergeant returned sharply, "everyone including Catholics deserves civil rights and that's the cause of our problem. If the minority had basic rights we wouldn't be in this mess." The big man exploded in a fit of rage smashing his glass on the counter. "Are you fucking mad policeman, look what happened when we gave the darkies in India civil liberties, they rose above their station and you want us to give them Taigs civil rights, second class citizens deserve second class rights and that's the way it's always been in Ulster and that's the way it's going to stay? And by the way, Taig lover, I forgot to ask, how's that sweet little wife of yours, what do you call her now, Eileen, that's it; you kept that one quiet, sergeant. So, one of our own, a member of our Ulster security forces goes and marries a fuckin` terrorist. But...," he hesitated, "oh, sorry, sergeant, she's a dead Taig now, isn't she? I read her memorial in the Irish News, we read the Taig newspapers to find out the personal details of the terrorists we eliminate and get all the gory details. The lads get great satisfaction out of that and we like to check the Mass times in case the boys want to leave a little unholy surprise for the Taigs on a Sunday morning if you get my meaning." He laughed. "Poor Eileen, well, one less to worry about as the wise man says, the only good Taig is a dead one. So, Sergeant Murray, if you're missing your Taig wife that much I can have the boys dig her up and leave her corpse on the couch waiting for you tonight when you come home with your Chinese takeaway and bottle of Black Bush, you're fond of the Black Bush aren't you now, sergeant." Stepping forward, the sergeant slammed his fist hard into the big man's face smashing his glasses and knocking him to the floor, blood spurting from a broken nose. "Taig lover," the big man screamed, "the best is yet to come, the boys have only started just wait and see." "Are you okay, sergeant," the constable inquired, "you look like you've seen a ghost." "Maybe I have," replied the sergeant, "maybe I have." As they drove back to the station a multitude of thoughts raced through his mind. *If I made one serious mistake in my life, it was not going to Canada the time I was offered that job in the Canadian Mounted Police only Eileen wouldn't leave her family in the west of the city. We should have gone and left all this death and destruction behind, I can't see any end to the awful mess!*

A Chinese takeaway or fish and chips were the sergeant's thoughts as he drove out of the police station after his twelve-hour shift. He stopped at the Chinese ordering a beef curry and fried rice, however, he didn't call at his normal off-license instead stopping at another further down the road; he'd developed a dislike for the shop assistant, Willie. He opened the front door, stepped into the hall, and closing the door behind him waited for the sound of her soft voice calling from the bedroom. "Home, at last, my big, handsome policeman, come up here now and show your wife how much you love her, and don't forget to take off those size tens." Eileen, his beloved wife, the love of his life, and now she's gone. It was all so sudden, one minute everything's grand, making passionate love before he went to work that fateful Saturday. She goes shopping with her sister Peggy and they go into a city centre bar for a drink when a no-warning bomb explodes killing them instantly. So swift and brutal, his poor wife, why her. She didn't deserve to die, so badly mutilated he could barely recognise her body. No organisation claimed responsibility, but did it matter who butchered her, they were all murdering bastards as far as he was concerned. He shuddered on entering the cold living room, tears of bitterness running down his cheeks, eyes strained in the darkness as he bent down turning on the two-bar electric heater and reaching over switched on the television. He sat back heavily on the couch without taking off his coat, pulled off his boots, placing his service revolver on the table, eating his beef curry with a dirty fork while drinking a large measure of Black Bush from an unwashed glass and when finished slouched back, snoring gently, drifting into a deep slumber when a noise startled him. *That bloody milkman again, rattling those damn milk bottles. I'll have to have a word with him one of these days.* He listened carefully; it was the low purring hum of a diesel engine, the reverberation rattling the single pane of glass in the sliding sash timber living room window. He grabbed his revolver and cocking the weapon crept silently to the window. A republican hit squad; he always knew they would come for him, only a matter of time, and parting the curtains stepped back in stunned silence. A double-decker bus sat outside overshadowing his house, its running engine murmuring low and soft, its lights turned off. *It's a bomb* was his immediate reaction, but when he looked again he could make out dark figures silhouetted against the neon glow of the streetlights, sitting on the upper and lower decks: the bus was full. *Jesus Christ, what the hell is a packed bus doing outside my house at three o clock in the morning?* He opened the front door and peered outside, nothing; the street empty except for the double-decker towering menacingly over the property, the door open but the driver's seat empty. Clambering aboard an eerie spectacle confronted Sergeant Murray. The bus was full of men and boys who sat silent and motionless, mannequin-like, staring blankly ahead. He approached two figures at the front and focused hard stepping back in horror; their throats were cut. He stood petrified on a bus full of corpses sitting together frozen in death. Wheeling around, he staggered towards the door gasping for breath, slipping and sliding on the viscous mess. Jumping onto the pavement, he could see the face of the big man glowering at him, pint in hand. *Kill all Taigs and let God sort them out.* Stumbling into the house he slammed the door shut, his body shaking uncontrollably, and collapsing onto the couch with trembling hands filled the tumbler to overflowing finishing the whiskey in one gulp and placing the revolver to his temple uttered. *Eileen, I'm coming to visit you in heaven* as he pulled the trigger. The inspector and the constable stood over the crumpled body of the sergeant, the remnants of the leftover blood-tainted curry and the revolver lying on the floor. The inspector noticed something. "What's that he`s holding, constable, see what it is?" The constable handed the inspector a blood-covered, black and white photograph, which he wiped with his handkerchief to reveal the faded image of a young smiling couple arm in arm on their wedding day, the handsome man wearing the uniform of a police officer.

And so, Sergeant John Murray, leaving behind his cold house with the faint smell of damp and decay, unwashed glasses, dirty cutlery, and a half-full bottle of Black Bush whiskey on the coffee table, has gone forever to visit his beloved Eileen in heaven!

THE END